Jacob Jennings

A Novel of the Texas Frontier

By Jack L Knapp

Jacob Jennings

By the Author:

The Wizards Series

Combat Wizard
Wizard at Work
Talent
The Wizards Series Boxed Set (Combat Wizard, Wizard at Work, and Talent)
Veil of Time
Siberian Wizard
Magic
Angel (A Wizards Short Story)

The Darwin's World Series

Darwin's World
The Trek
Home
Boxed Set, the Darwin's World Series (Darwin's World, The Trek, and Home)
The Return
Defending Eden

The New Frontiers Series

The Ship
NFI: New Frontiers, Inc
NEO: Near Earth Objects
The New Frontiers Series Boxed Set (The Ship, NFI, and NEO)
BEMs: Bug Eyed Monsters
MARS: The Martian Autonomous Republic of Sol
Pirates

Historic Western

The Territory: A Novel of the American West
Jacob Jennings: A Novel of the Texas Frontier

Novella

Hands

Want a free book? Drop a note listing typos or similar errors to jlknapp505@msn.com. Identify the error by copy-pasting the sentence it occurs in and suggest an improvement. I'll be happy to gift you a free ebook, your choice of any I've published.

COPYRIGHT

Jacob Jennings

A Novel of the Texas Frontier

Copyright © 2020 by Jack L Knapp
Cover Photo, Print Edition, by Jack L Knapp

Table of Contents

Chapter One

I had no idea that when the three dusty, tired-looking riders rode up to Uncle Horace's farmhouse that summer of 1828 my life was about to change again.

"Welcome, Harry!" Uncle Horace said. "I was afraid my letter would get to your place in Alexandria while you were off in Texas! Light and set!"

That was more words than I'd heard from Uncle Horace in the past two months, ever since the rains came and the river overflowed. That's how I knew that the visitors were important.

I looked on curiously, never having seen them before, but Uncle Horace clearly knew them well.

I suddenly remembered that my pa had mentioned a brother named Harold. I'd never met him and the one time I'd asked, Pa had hesitated before answering. "We don't see much of Harry, Jake. Your ma doesn't like having him around. He associates with bad companions, for one, and he drinks more'n he ought to. I figured it was easier to not ruffle her feathers."

That brief explanation and the look on his face had made me curious enough to ask my cousin Pete during our fishing trip east to the Red River. "He's the family black sheep, Jakey! Every family has one, seems like, and he's ours!"

That led to a friendly tussle and I'd thought to ask my pa what Pete had meant after I got home, but I never got the chance. Two days later, before we returned from that fishing trip, a tornado tore its way through our farm. The house was ripped apart down to the foundation and when I got back, I found my Uncle Horace waiting to tell me that I was an orphan.

It took a few minutes before it hit me, that I was alone in the world. No family, and me still a kid! Where would I live? Would anybody give me a job?

I'd seen orphans a time or two and felt sorry for them, ragged and homeless as they were. They sure-enough had a hard life. Did they live by begging?

But then Uncle Horace continued, so I knowed I wouldn't starve.

"You'll be going with us, Jake. My brothers and me talked about it and decided that the best thing to do was to just join Hiram's property to mine. I reckon it'll be yours one day, when you're old enough."

Not that it was ever going to be worth much, far as I could tell. Seemed like the river flooded every two years or so, and soggy fields won't grow much of anything except crawdads. They're good for catfish bait, but not much else.

But thinking about what had happened back then didn't take long, and I found myself wondering: could this really be my Uncle Harry?

But I didn't have to wonder long. "These must be my nephews Matthew and Mark!" said Uncle Horace. "I haven't seen you two since you were tots! Say howdy to your cousin Jake, boys!"

I took a closer look at them while they sized me up. Uncle Harry had a patch of white in his hair and wrinkles around his eyes, while Matthew and Mark looked to be twins, grown men who wouldn't be interested in a 14-year-old poor-relation. I left them to their talk and climbed my favorite tree to look out across the empty fields and think.

After dark, when the catching-up was done, Uncle Harry called me in. I had been leaning against the corral, admiring their horses and wishing I had one for my own. Not that *that* was likely to happen, poor as we were. I looked around for Uncle Horace, but I reckon he was off with my aunt figuring out how to feed his guests.

Things had been mighty slim lately. The rabbits and such we caught by trapping helped feed us, and Pete and me ran trot lines too. Uncle Horace sold the catfish we caught and used the money to buy flour and beans.

Then I remembered that he still had some cured bacon and two hams left from the butchering last fall. Maybe that was where he was, in the smokehouse.

Uncle Harry interrupted my wool-gathering. "You'll bunk in the barn tonight with my boys, Jake," he said. "Tomorrow, we'll see about a horse for you. Can you ride? Not just farm plugs, but really ride? Spend all day in the saddle?"

"I've ridden the wheel-horse while we were snaking logs out of the woods," I confessed, "but nothing like you're talking about. I'm really going with you? And I'm to have a horse of my own?"

"You are, Son. Horace took you in after Hi was killed and 'twas a good thing he did, but he can't keep you now. He's got problems enough just feeding his own family and next year is likely to be worse. We brought a little money for him, enough for him to pay off his debts and buy supplies during the winter, but things are still going to be tight. You'll be better off with us."

"I knowed he was having trouble," I agreed. "Last year and the year before that, I would have been out in the fields by now picking peas and beans or plowing up potato rows. But since the river washed out the crops, Pete and me have been trapping and fishing just to keep the family fed."

"Trapping," Uncle Harry was clearly not impressed by what we'd done. "'Coons and possums, Boy, judging by supper. Can you shoot?"

"No, sir; I never learned. But I'd prefer you call me Jake, Uncle Harry. I've been doing a man's work since Uncle Horace took me in."

He grinned at me and my cousins chuckled. "Feisty, you are! Wal, your daddy Hi was the same way! He'd fight a feller at the drop of a hat, and often enough it was the other feller's hat he dropped! We'll get along, young Jake!"

I helped my cousins lay out quilts on the hay for our beds and we were soon asleep. But not for long; Uncle Harry shook us awake before daybreak.

During the night, someone had brought a half-broke mustang in and turned it into the small corral out back. I didn't know it then, but Uncle Harry dealt in Mexican mustangs; all he'd needed to do was pass on to his partner in Alexandria that he needed one with spirit and lots of bottom.

I helped with saddling the ones they'd ridden the day before, but avoided that mean-looking, wall-eyed bronc, wondering how I was going to keep up when they left.

My cousins noticed my expression. "You'll ride my horse, Jake," said Mark. "I'll get acquainted with this critter, and by the time we get to the Sabine he'll know who's boss!"

I was plumb relieved to hear that! But we didn't go there right away. Uncle Harry had a nice place just outside of Alexandria and that's where we spent the next few days, with me busy learning to ride and shoot.

He gave me a smoothbore musket and a brace of pistols that took the new percussion caps; they'd belonged to my cousin Matt before he got new weapons to replace them. Uncle Horace owned a musket and a shotgun and I'd shot both, but powder was in short supply.

Just as well, far as I was concerned; that musket had bruised my shoulder black-and-blue the one time I'd shot it and the shotgun had knocked me on my butt. But that had been back when I was still a boy of less than ten years. I reckoned that I could shoot a man's weapon now.

Turned out I was right. While Uncle Harry met with people he did business with, my cousins taught me how to shoot. My new musket and pistol, but also a double-barreled shotgun and Matt's new rifle, the first one I'd seen.

I tried my best to hit the targets they'd set up, but I couldn't help flinching. Every time I jerked the trigger, the sights drifted away from the target so that the bullet kicked up dirt three feet to the right!

I could tell right off that my cousins were thinking I was never going to amount to much, and maybe they were right.

But after every miss, I refused to rub my sore shoulder like I wanted. Instead, I pulled the ramrod out of its thimbles and swabbed out the barrel, then poured in a full powder charge. They watched me and understood. Reducing the powder charge would have caused the guns to kick less, but I knowed how disappointed they already were in me and refused.

4

Even though every time I shot, it felt like I was stabbing my sore shoulder with a knife.

Between all the shooting we did in the morning and riding cross-country for long stretches in the afternoon, I was so sore when we turned in at night that I wondered if I would be able to sleep. But I always did, and woke up the next morning stiff and sore to do it all over again.

Except for shooting Matt's rifle; that only happened once.

It was a pretty thing, all curly maple in the stock and with a perfectly-browned and oiled barrel and lock. I would have shot it again because it didn't kick nearly as hard, but he claimed I wouldn't need to shoot a rifle during the trips we would be making. I would be armed with pistols and a musket, so if I could learn to shoot them that was all that was needful. I think he just liked to keep that rifle for himself. Jealous, the way I figured it.

I also met Uncle Harry's two slaves. They would go on the next trip with us. "Jake, Pa and Matt and me will be out ahead, scouting for trouble," Mark explained. "You'll follow half a mile or so behind us.

"You'll be in charge of our string of mules, but mind that you listen to Tom and his boy Isom. When they tell you something needs doing, you *do* it, and with no back talk, understand? Tom's family has been part of our family for years and his wife Maudie raised Matt and me!

"He knows as much about the trips we make as we do, nearly. Isom's still learning but he already knows a lot more than you, so you listen to him too."

I said I would, and thought nothing of it at the time. They weren't the first colored folks I'd seen, and Pa would have taken his belt to me if I had ever treated a grownup one disrespectful. *He* might have called them by name, but to me they were all 'Uncle' or 'Aunt' unless they were really old. After that, I could say 'Grandfather' or 'Grandmother' and nobody thought nothing of it.

"Something else you should know," Matt said. "As soon as we cross the Sabine, we'll be in Texas. Being as it's part of Mexico, owning slaves ain't allowed over there, but don't you worry. They'll stick by us because like I said, they're part of the family.

You understand what I'm saying? You're green as a magnolia leaf, but they've already been on more'n a dozen trips with us. And every time that we crossed the Sabine, they knowed just as we did that every man's hand was against us. We won't be safe until we reach friends in San Augustine, and maybe not then."

"I understand, Mark," I said. "What will the mules be packing?"

"Usual cargo," Mark said. "Coffee, whiskey, and tobacco for the most part. We can buy it cheaper on this side of the river and sell it for more over in Texas, what the Mexican government calls smuggling.

"Their customs officers collect a tax on them when they come in by port, which makes them more expensive. Uncle Henry is in the same business as us, except he anchors his barkentine out by Campeche Island and lands his cargoes after dark.

"Part of your job if we run into trouble is to take care of Tom and Isom. Any number of planters across that river came from Louisiana or another place where slavery is still legal, and if they could get their hands on ours we might never see them again. I would purely hate to tell Aunt Maudie that you let them take her family!

"You understand? If a stranger should come around and show interest in Tom or Isom, well, that's why we're teaching you to shoot. We *expect* you to, if you're up to it. Killing a man, I mean."

"I'll do what's needful," I said shortly. "I'm to do what you said before, shoot first, and if I have any questions ask them afterwards?"

"That's it, Jake," Mark said grimly. "Don't try to scare him, don't try to just wound him. Shoot to kill, and reload as fast as you can after you shoot 'cause there's likely to be more than one.

He relaxed a little after that and went on. "It probably won't happen, because we know the trails and like I said, we'll be out in front scouting, but a body never knows. And not just slavers, Jake; Mexicans will hang us if they catch us, and the Indians…wal, don't let 'em take you alive. Save one of the pistols for yourself.

"Tom and Isom, they know. They'll run for it if the Indians

catch us and generally they don't have all that much to fear from the Tonks, seeing as they're black. But being as you're white, Indians will either kill you or turn you over to their women for torture. Do what you have to, but *don't* let them take you alive!"

Lots to think about. I sure hoped we didn't run into any wild Indians over there in Texas!

***

That first trip went off without a hitch, so I figured Mark knowed what he was talking about.

Eight days after leaving Alexandria, we slipped into San Augustine and met Uncle Harry's Texian partners, Antonio Leal and Philip Nolan. Nolan had property there, including the corrals where he kept the wild mustangs that had been rounded up by Mister Leal and his employees.

We swapped our mules and their cargoes for a herd of mustangs and some money. Uncle Harry carried that on the way back and scouted out ahead, while Mark and Matt helped me and the slaves with the mustangs.

We were all tired by the time we got back to Alexandria and turned them into Uncle Harry's corrals. They would remain there until sold, which likely wouldn't take more than a day or two, but other people would handle that. My cousins and me would take a day off to rest, and after that they had promised to take me hunting and maybe a few other places they knowed about too.

As soon as money from the sale of the horses started to come in, Uncle Harry started buying:

Whiskey from Arkansas and Tennessee, French brandy that had been smuggled into New Orleans, coffee from Africa, dried bales of leaf tobacco from Alabama and the Carolinas, and anything else he thought would turn a profit after we'd smuggled it into Mexican Texas, keeping in mind that everything had to be transported on mules.

Muskets, rifles, and lead bars for making bullets turned a healthy profit, but because of their weight and length they came by sea.

***

Unlike farming, which was a year to year thing, smuggling paid very well so Uncle Harry was a rich and respected man in Alexandria.

I met many of his friends and acquaintances who stopped by, including a man named James Bowie. "You watch out for him, Jake," said Matt. "Pa and him were in business years ago, along with a Frenchman named Jean Lafitte, and a dirty business it was.

"Lafitte was a pirate before he joined up with Andy Jackson at the Battle of New Orleans. He got a pardon after that, him and his right-hand man Dominique You. He's turned respectable, You has, but Lafitte...wal, that rascal's still a pirate if he ain't been hung yet! As for Bowie, he'd kill you as soon as look at you!

"That knife he always carries? He's famous for it. He won't talk about what he's done, but I hear tell he's gutted a dozen men with it! One of 'em had stuck a sword in his chest and it was still hanging out when Bowie knifed him!"

I filed that information away, because Mister Bowie seemed nothing like the dangerous character Matt said he was. But just to be on the safe side, I was always as polite to him as he was to me and my uncle and cousins.

***

Weather permitting, we made two or three trips every summer after Uncle Harry took me in.

I learned a lot during that time, got used to riding long hours at night, and enjoyed being part of my uncle's family. If there was a single issue that bothered me, it was that the better families wouldn't allow me to associate with their daughters. Turned out that respect among men didn't carry over to families!

Matt and Mark found other outlets, and as I grew older, so did I.

I had no wish to get married anyway. Girls either married by 16 or were thought of as old maids. Men, not so much. Just as well, far as I was concerned. The few young women I met knowed lots of stuff I'd never heard of and as soon as they found out how dumb I was, they tended to smirk at me. If they'd have been boys—well, men my age—I'd have shown them a thing or two, because I was no slouch with my fists.

But being as they were girls, it was easier just to not be around them.

***

There was increasing tension across the Sabine, starting around 1830. By 1831 and on into 1832, the troubles that had started down in Mexico had spread to Texas.

An insurrection was brewing down there, and a new name was being spoken of, Antonio Lopez de Santa Anna. A coming man, folks said.

There were disagreements between Mexican government officials and the American settlers who favored Santa Anna, as well as between Mexican authorities and the illegal settlers that had crossed to take up land without permission. Unlike Steven Austin's Old Three Hundred, many just crossed the Sabine River, picked a likely spot out in the woods, and started clearing land. Others didn't bother doing even that much; they set up tents along the trails and started trading. More'n one little town had started that way, according to Matt.

We talked now and then about doing the same thing, my cousins and me. Smuggling was growing more dangerous all the time, and nowadays it didn't pay as well as before. Uncle Harry was ready to quit too, but he wasn't sure what he would do afterwards. He owned property in Arkansas as well as Louisiana and mentioned one day that he might take up land speculating, maybe with Jim Bowie and his brother Rezin.

But he would need more money if he intended to go into that business in a big way.

One, maybe two more smuggling trips might be enough.

***

I didn't much care for the ferryman's attitude when we crossed the Sabine, but when I mentioned it to Uncle Harry he dismissed it.

"Times are tough and I reckon he's having money trouble, what with not many wanting to cross nowadays. But we'll keep our eyes peeled and you remember what I told you, don't be too slow to shoot and take care of Tom and Isom. If it comes down to you and them or the mules, wal, cache the cargo if you have time and find a thicket to hide in. Mules ain't cheap but family is dear, and a man can always buy more mules."

I nodded, and we headed west.

I paid close attention to the trail, which unlike our earlier trips hadn't seen much traffic since the last rain. Between that and how that ferryman had acted, I was nervous.

Not afraid, because my cousins hat taught me that while a man might be concerned now and then, he wasn't never afraid. So I wasn't, but I was concerned enough that I checked the priming on my pistols and that old musket.

I heard Tom murmuring to Isom after he saw me doing that, but I was too far ahead to hear what they were saying. I figured that they were as concerned as I was.

When I heard that first gunshot up ahead of us, I pulled up and held my hand up to signal Tom and Isom to halt the mules. We waited for half a minute, then there was another shot. It was followed by a dozen loud booms and a lot of yelling.

The first two shots had cracked the way my family's rifles did; the others were dull booms that sounded like muskets. It concerned me—I wasn't afraid, I was concerned—but I knew what I had to do, so I got to it.

"Tom, you and Isom lead the mules over by that thicket. Don't take the time to unpack, just unfasten the girths and dump the saddles where they might not be spotted. As soon as you've done that, turn the mules loose and the two of you head back to that swamp we passed a few minutes ago. The edges are thick with reeds, so if you can make it to that hummock out in the middle you ought to be safe."

"What about you, Marse Jake?" asked Tom anxiously.

"I'm going to wait a few minutes right here to see if Uncle Harry or my cousins got away. They might be wounded, and if they are they'll need help."

"Marse Jake, all that yelling; it sounded Spanish to me," Isom said.

"Me too, Isom," I admitted, "but my uncle and the boys, they're family. You are too, comes to that, and it might be that all I can do for you is slow up whoever it was that ambushed my uncle.

"But in case I don't make it…well, Tom, you take care of yourself and Isom. Just you two, don't concern yourself about me or the rest of us. The horses…you can't let them whinny if they scent another horse, so be ready to pinch their nostrils closed. Turn them loose if you have to.

"You two take care of yourselves and I'll be along directly." I would have cussed at letting my mouth run away like that if I hadn't been trying to be quiet!

A little bit later, I found a big magnolia to hide behind and waited. An hour passed, as long a time as I ever spent and as concerned as I ever want to be. But finally, the forest woke up and gradually started to sound normal, with birdsongs and rustlings from small critters. And after a bit longer, off in the distance where the gunshots had sounded, a squirrel chattered.

When I heard that, I knowed that whatever had happened was over. So I gave up waiting and headed back along the way we'd come, keeping a lookout for the hummock where I expected to find Tom and Isom.

Chapter Two

We spent a warm night out in the swamp, waving away mosquitoes because we were too concerned about making noise to swat them. Way off in the distance, I heard alligators grunting. I reckoned that they weren't as concerned as us. But nothing important happened that night, despite us spooking at every close-by rustle of the reeds when a coon or some other critter passed by.

We were all hungry next morning but there were blackberries in every clearing, ripe and as long and thick as the end of my thumb. We ate as many as we thought safe, knowing that too many will give a man the runs. There were also more frogs in that swamp than a body could ever catch, so I knowed that we wouldn't starve.

Isom knew how to capture them by splitting the small end of a cane pole back to the first joint, then carefully carving a kind of spike behind the sharpened points so the frog couldn't wiggle his way off. It worked on a cottonmouth too, but I left that one to Tom and Isom to eat. I was a mite hungry, but not *that* hungry!

When I was sure we were alone, I gave Tom permission to build a fire while I kept watch to make sure I hadn't missed anything. A body can't be too careful, Uncle Harry had said, but I wondered. Maybe he hadn't been careful enough.

After Tom got the fire going, they cooked what they'd caught while I headed afoot back to where I'd last seen my uncle and my cousins. Took me the best part of two hours, because I was being careful, but I homed on buzzards circling in the sky and found my uncle and my cousins.

The Mexicans had hung their dead bodies from a tree limb as a warning to others.

Uncle Harry had been shot several times, including one that had taken off part of his skull. Matt had also been shot and either lanced or knifed in the body, while Mark had died from having his throat cut after he'd been shot. I cut them down and was trying to figure what to do with the bodies when Tom and Isom slipped out of the woods.

"You keep watch, Marse Jake. We'll take care of your uncle and his boys.

"There ain't no reason to go back to where we was; we swung by where we'd left the packs on the way here and they were gone, the mules too. I reckon the Mexicans found them, which might be why they didn't come looking for us."

My throat was tight, so I just nodded my gratitude to Tom and went off to the far side of the clearing to do what he'd said.

I watched the leaves and Spanish moss hang sad from the trees while they scraped out shallow graves by the side of the trail. It was more than I could have done working by myself and after they were finished, we mounted up and headed south down a deer trail. I didn't feel like talking and I reckon they didn't either. They'd known Uncle Harry and my cousins a lot longer than I had, depended on them just like I had and like we had depended on each other during the trips.

A part of their lives had ended when my uncle was killed, just like part of mine had.

There had still been a little bit of being a kid in me up to yesterday, a sense of adventure and more than a little bravado because we were outwitting the Mexican authorities. Now, whatever was left of that was back there in that lonely clearing where Tom and Isom had buried my folks.

A lot of responsibility had landed on my shoulders, so I done a lot of thinking while I rode along. I scanned the trail and the woods, but I also watched my horse's ears. I knowed that he would spot trouble before I would.

I didn't have a lot of choices, and the ones I had weren't worth thinking about. I glanced back a time or two at Tom and Isom, wondering if they were as worried as I was, but if they were they didn't show it so I didn't either.

By and by, I straightened up and tried to look like I knew where we were going. Boys can shuck worries, but a man faces up to his responsibilities. He's allowed to worry, I reckon—I certainly did—but I didn't show it, any more than Uncle Harry would have.

The thought came on, all surprising. Had Uncle Harry ever worried like I was doing? And never allowed it to show, so that I wouldn't *have* to worry?

I missed him already, my cousins too.

There would be no forgetting what those Mexican soldiers had done to their bodies. I felt like cussing and had thoughts of someday doing to them what they'd done to my family, but it was only idle thoughts trying to chase bad memories away.

Underneath was the knowing that *they* did what they did because we did what *we* did, and there was an end to it.

***

Later that afternoon, I heard turkeys gobbling up ahead.

A rifle might be accurate enough to fetch a turkey, but an old smoothbore musket? Half a dozen shot would do reliably what a ball wouldn't, so I drew the ball from my musket and reloaded with shot. That done, I checked the cap to make sure it hadn't shifted while I worked. Hungry as we were, it wouldn't do to be careless!

Finally, as ready as I was ever going to get, I snuck up closer to the turkeys. Seemed like these had never been hunted before; they weren't nearly as spooky as the ones over in Louisiana! I shot a big old gobbler and he barely kicked after he fell out of that nesting tree.

Isom drew the entrails while I reloaded with powder and ball, and he carried the turkey when we rode on south looking for a place to hide. A mile further on, I spotted the entrance to a thicket that looked about as good as any. Tom started a fire while Isom headed for a nearby creek and cut several canes that were thick enough to hold the meat while it cooked.

Even without salt, that turkey tasted far better than what we'd eaten the night before, and hungry as we were we ate him down to the bone.

While we relaxed after supper, I shared my thinking with Tom and Isom.

"We'd have been asking for trouble if we'd gone on to San

Augustine. No telling where those soldiers went; they might have loaded the packs on our mules and sold them to the same people we figured to sell to, but they also might have split up and only sent one or two in. The rest could still be out there patrolling."

Tom nodded understanding, so I went on.

"Even if we got there, we wouldn't find friends. Leal and Nolan were Uncle Harry's business partners, but they're not ours because we don't have anything to trade. For that matter, *they* might be dead by now because buying smuggled cargoes is likely just as illegal as bringing them in.

"Heading back east is out too. I expect we got caught because the ferryman warned that detachment to watch for us, maybe by sending a rider. Slow as the mules were, he would have had plenty of time to reach them and let them know we were coming.

"As for going north, I have no idea what's up that way but I've heard that the Indians aren't friendly. That leaves south, all the way to Galveston. Uncle Henry needs to know what happened to his brother and nephews. Another thing, he's captain of his own ship so he might have a job for me, or at least be able to tell me where to start looking. What do you think?"

"What about us, Marse Jake?" asked Tom softly.

"I got a duty to care for you," I admitted, "You've been like family, but being honest, I ain't sure I can even take care of myself. All I can promise is that I'll do my best. We're in Texas and slavery's against the law here, just like it is in the rest of Mexico, meaning that you're free to go your own way and take your chances if that's your choice. Galveston is a pretty big place from what I hear. You could get jobs there and I think you'd be safe.

"Tom, I don't know if it will help, but as soon as we get somewhere that I can find paper and pen I'll write out a statement that you bought freedom for yourself and your family. Over here, probably no one will question it. Shucks, you might not ever be asked to show it. But if you head back to Louisiana, I just don't know what would happen."

"It's a big step, Marse Jake. Marse Harry offered to free us, all of us, years ago, but a paper don't stop a man with a gun from putting a rope on us and selling us all over again. What if we was to go on to Galveston with you? You write out that paper for me when we get there and do what you can for Isom, but I can't just up and leave the rest of my family back in Louisiana.

"Would you let me have the horses after we get to Galveston? I reckon that if I ride after dark and lay up during the day, I can reach Alexandria in a week or two. After that, I'll collect up my wife and the children and try to join up with you in Galveston."

"You're welcome to them, Tom," I said, and I felt half of my load fall right off. "I've got a few dollars put aside and you can have those too. I only wish I could do more. If you want to wait around until the next time Uncle Henry is in port, I'll ask him if he can do more than I can to help you."

"No, I don't think I can wait," he said. "No telling what might happen to my family when folks find out that your uncle and his boys are dead. If you're willing to give me one of your pistols, that might help after I get back there."

"I'll do that right now," I said. "You know how to shoot?"

Isom snickered and Tom just winked, so I took that as a yes.

Over in Louisiana it wasn't acceptable, and if they had found out some of Uncle Harry's neighbors would have fallen down and had a foaming fit! But he hadn't paid a whole lot of attention to what others thought, and I made up my mind right then that his way of thinking was good enough for me.

**

Two days later, we reached a big river.

We hid back in the woods and talked it over. "It's flowing south and we're on the eastern bank," I said, "so it can't be the Sabine. It might be the Neches, but if it is and we follow it south, we might run into the Sabine again. We'd be worse off if that was to happen than we are now. Whichever one it is, the farther south we go, the bigger it's going to get. I wonder if we could make a raft?"

"Not one big enough to hold the horses, Marse Jake," Tom said. "If we had an axe or a saw…"

"But we don't, Tom," I said. "We might have to abandon the

horses and go the rest of the way on foot." I could tell he didn't like that idea, counting on the horses as he was, but while we might be able to cross by holding on to a floating log, the horses would drown if we tried to take them with us.

"Maybe not," said Isom, pointing upstream. "Look at that boat way up yonder. Or maybe it's a raft, I can't rightly tell from here. But see if you can make out the man holding on to the tiller."

I did, and from what I could see, he was as black as Tom or Isom. "Freedman, you think?" I asked.

"I'd bet on it," said Tom, "either that, or he's a runaway from Louisiana.

"People cut logs and tie 'em together back there, then float them downriver to market. I've never been on one, but I've heard tell how it's done and I've seen 'em on the Red River east of Alexandria.

"I can try to hail him, if that's okay with you."

I said yes, so he did. "Howdy, the boat!" he yelled.

The man holding on to the steering pole jumped and looked around. I wondered if he had been half asleep. But he woke up, and Tom hollered that we had run into trouble up north and needed help.

There was some talk back and forth while that raft drifted closer, but finally the boatman agreed.

"I'll throw you a rope from the bow," he called out. "You wrap it around one of those big trees and hang on. Don't tie it, mind you; I've only got the one rope and I don't want to have to cut part of it away to get loose!"

Isom did as the boatman said, and with his help Tom and me loaded our horses. They'd crossed on ferries a number of times, so while they took some convincing we eventually got it done. Isom let go of the rope and jumped on board as the raft started drifting away.

Me and him took care of the animals while Tom went back to help with the steering. We listened to them talk, but mostly it was the man who owned the raft that did the talking while Tom listened. "There's a ferry that crosses the river about ten miles south of here and a road that will take you west. First time in this part of the country?" he asked.

Tom said it was and told him we wanted to get to Galveston.

"Then you're better off taking the next road that goes south. There are other ferries, so if you just stay on the road you'll get there if you got money to pay. The Neches and the Sabine both end up at a bay that opens out on to the Gulf," he said, "but I'll sell my raft before I get that far south and head back upriver. Time I get home, my boys will have more timbers waiting. Spend a few days with my wife and family, then do it again. Ain't a bad living if you're a mind to work, and as long as you stay west of the Sabine you're safe enough.

"Watch yourself when you get close to the Gulf. The Tonkawas are generally friendly, not that I'd be overly trusting of any, but the Karankawas are cannibals. Ain't many left nowadays, but a body can't be too careful."

Good advice, I figured. I'd heard it often enough from Uncle Harry!

After a while, Tom and Isom took turns relieving the man on the steering oar while he slept. It seemed like he hadn't had a wink for several days, and maybe he hadn't. He might have just dozed off now and then and woke up long enough to keep his raft between the banks.

Late that afternoon, he steered close to a point that stuck out into the river. Isom jumped on shore and snubbed the rope around a big oak tree and we took our leave of the raftsman. We waved our thanks as he steered back into the channel and he waved back.

We watered the animals—they hadn't had a proper drink while we were on the raft—and let them graze for a while. As soon as the boss gelding stopped grazing where he was and went to chasing the others off what they were eating, I figured they'd had enough and we moved on.

An hour or so later, we found a place to camp. Good water, lots of fallen oak branches, and plenty of rank grass for the horses to graze on.

I kept watch with my musket ready, Tom built the fire, and Isom set out traps. Just before dark he brought in a big rabbit and a large bird of some kind. Along with some persimmons we'd gathered along the way, they were enough to satisfy our hunger.

I bit into one that wasn't quite ripe and as soon as I puckered up, I could see that Tom and Isom were trying to keep still. But after I got control enough to grin at them, they both busted out laughing. Persimmons are mighty tasty when they're ripe, but a body needs to know how to keep them until they get that way. If you wait for them to ripen on the tree, the possums will have 'em before you know it. The thing to do is to pick them before they're ripe enough to interest the possums and put them in the flour barrel until they turn ripe.

Uncle Horace's wife had taught me that, and a lot more besides!

After the fire was out, I moved out into the darkness and tried to ignore the skeeters. I finally cut a palmetto branch and waved that slowly around my face. In the darkness, moving it around like that was safe enough I figured, and it sure did make life harder for the pesky things!

About midnight I woke up Isom and handed over the musket. I was so tired that I don't remember going to sleep, but I 'spect I must have.

Tom shook me awake just before dawn.

Chapter Three

Galveston was raw; there was no other word for it, compared with Alexandria, which had a number of fine buildings and an air of permanence. If Galveston had any such, I couldn't see them from where we had stopped close to the customs house.

I had given Tom one of my pistols, choosing to keep the other. Now I handed the musket to Isom, along with my bag of shot and the powder horn, and went inside.

The single large room had a table toward the back and several taller tables close to the front where two people were standing, writing. I marveled at how fast they worked, hardly pausing at all. An older man that was sitting at a table in back looked at me, not saying anything at first.

I couldn't blame him; after weeks on the trail surviving off what we could eat and with no chance to clean up except when we got rained on, I sure didn't cut a respectable figure.

But I straightened up and walked over.

"Señor?" he asked.

"You speak American, Sir?" I responded. My Spanish had more gaps than a picket-shed's wall, which might lead to misunderstandings I had no need of.

"English, French, the language of my country, and if necessary a translator of Portuguese can be found. You have business with Mexico?"

I explained as much as I could without lying more than necessary. The upshot was that he wrote out the papers of manumission for me and I signed 'em. He even put a nice stamp on them, which I couldn't read but it sure dressed the papers up!

Cost me more than a body would expect, but I reckon that's how governments make money. Or maybe it was how he made a living; I wondered if he'd knowed exactly how much money I had when he decided what to charge me, because at the end I had almost none.

I turned the papers over to Tom and apologized that I no longer had money to give him, but he allowed that he'd make out. He took the reins and hugged Isom while I turned away to avoid seeing tears in their eyes. If it had been anyone else except these two, I might have thought it unmanly.

But I listened to Tom's instructions to Isom, and then I worried more. "You help Marse Jake, Son. He's got more nerve than a body would expect, knowing his age, and I 'spect he'll do as much or more than I could to take care of you. I'll look for you when I get back, although it might take me two or three months. Maudie and your sisters, traveling after dark…well, we'll make out, but we'll have to be careful."

"I'll be okay, Pa," Isom said. "You take care of Ma, and when you get back put a notice on that big board in front of the customs house. Marse Jake and me'll keep an eye out."

Things got quiet for a bit, then I heard the creak of saddle leather when Tom mounted. I waited a while longer and by the time I turned, he was far enough away that I almost missed seeing him. But Isom was still watching, so I joined him until Tom followed a turn in the road and passed behind a building.

I reckon we made people wonder, me armed with pistol and knife, Isom half a step back of me with the musket, but nobody said anything. Maybe it was because most of the men we saw were armed, some better than us.

I asked around when we got closer to the port, not wanting to tell more than necessary, but we found people who knew of Captain Henry Jennings and the *Eureka* brigantine. "He'll get here when he gets here, young man. I know him well, and you resemble him enough to be related!"

I told the man I was, and that being newly-arrived, we were looking for work. He sent us off with a boy, who introduced us to a foreman who put us to work.

I wound up fetching and carrying, mostly planks for siding and floors, while Isom was put to work with the roofing crew.

I ain't sure which one of us got the worst job. Isom was

working up there in the sun, nailing cypress shakes in place while trying not to fall, while I ended up with sore muscles and more splinters from those oak boards than a body would believe. Not only in my hands, at least until I could afford gloves, but in my shoulders.

That evening, I sold the musket. It brought in enough to keep us fed and sheltered until we received our first pay.

We found lodgings that evening in a cheap boarding-house that catered mostly to sailors.

Unskilled workers, which is what we were, generally didn't stay in places like that, being more permanent. Some lived with family while they learned the trade, while others drank more bad whiskey than they ought to and there was no telling where they spent their nights. They might show up for work the next day or they might not.

Work started at daybreak and except for a short pause for us to eat, lasted until dark.

I thought that after we made a little more money, we might be able to move up in the world. There were better trades that a man could learn, and masters out on the frontier were always looking for hard-working apprentices or temporary helpers. All we'd need to do was save up our money and as soon as Tom got back, work our way out west and find someone who would teach us what we needed to know.

There was also free land to be had for the taking, so folks said, good bottom-land that would grow most anything a body could want. The government would insist on us joining the Catholic Church and learning the Spanish language before they would accept us as citizens, but others had done it. As for the Indians, they could be notional and a body had to keep a close eye on his livestock, especially horses, but again, others knew the way of it and I figured I could learn too.

***

Five weeks later, a man with the look of the sea about him came up to me. "You were asking about Henry Jennings?" he inquired softly. I confessed that I was.

"I can take you to him," he said.

I yelled up to Isom to come on down and right then and there, we quit that building gang.

The foreman didn't much like it, but after arguing a while he paid us half a day's wages and we set off with the seaman. I expected we'd head for the wharf, but instead, he led off on a trail through the scrub near the dunes that protected the interior of the island. He didn't want to explain at first, but after I mentioned Captain Henry was my uncle he opened up. Turns out he was coxswain of *Eureka*'s longboat.

"We don't tie up at the wharf until after we've unloaded most of our cargo in Campeche, which is where we're going. Ain't much, just a place where longboats can come in and find people to carry things to the sheds, but it suits us. The sheds ain't much either, but the cargoes won't be there long. Always buyers waiting, y' see; the fishermen let them know when a ship is heading in with stuff the captain doesn't want to declare. Ten years ago, it was Jean Lafitte's base for his pirate raids and it ain't changed a whole lot since.

"The people that own the wharf charge more than Captain Henry's willing to pay, plus there's the customs duties that the Mexican agent collects on legal cargoes. By the time *Eureka* comes to anchor in the bay, she'll be riding light, meaning no customs duties to speak of. The captain will make sure that there's just enough. That way, the customs agent can collect enough to pay for his time and send a little on to keep his bosses down in Mexico City from asking questions. They know what we do and we know they know, but if people don't go bragging about things they ought to keep quiet about nobody stirs up trouble.

"We'll stick around for another week or two, just long enough for the crew to get a run ashore. Campeche and Galveston are both sailor-friendly, with people happy to take his money and show him a good time. We'll start loading cargo for New Orleans later this week, then head out. I reckon it's a good thing for you boys that I heard you were asking about us!"

***

Uncle Henry was shorter and stouter than Uncle Harry, who

had been whipsaw-lean, but otherwise resembled him.

He also didn't take much convincing that I was family after he got a good look at me, although he was curious about Isom until I explained.

His mouth got grim, lips thin and jaw clenched tight, when I told him how Uncle Harry and my cousins had died. "Harry knew the risks," he finally admitted. "I had a letter a while back and he mentioned quitting the business, but I'm not surprised that it caught up to him before he did. He was always a gambler, my brother. As for your father, I was sorry to hear that he'd died so young. Storm, was it?"

"A tornado, folks said," I explained. "I didn't see it because I was away on a fishing trip. Uncle Horace took me in after that."

"A sad business. I might be your only relation now, except for Harry's family. Horace got into some trouble, something to do with selling land that wasn't exactly what he claimed from what I heard. The sheriff mentioned that in a letter and said that somebody set fire to his house. He claimed to know who'd done it, but hadn't caught the man yet. And he might not; lots of folks one jump ahead of a Louisiana hanging show up here in Texas under a new name.

"I'm sorry to tell you that I can't offer you money to live on. I carry just enough on board to pay my hands when we reach port; everything else is done through my agents on shore. What I *can* do is sign you both on. If you're willing to work, that is, and if you're not, well, the bos'n has his ways. I don't pay more attention to what he does and how he does it than is right and proper.

"Just so you know what you're letting yourself in for, sailing can be dangerous anywhere and the Gulf is as bad as any. There are hurricanes and pirates to look out for, and that's not mentioning the simple falls and ruptures that plague the hands. Some can't learn the trade and some get tired of the work and go ashore, so we're always looking to take on likely young men."

I glanced at Isom and he nodded.

"We'll sign, Uncle, and thank you." Uncle Henry nodded, then led us back to his cabin and signed us in on his muster book, with a last instruction before he turned us over to the bos'n.

"Let that be the last time you refer to me on this ship as 'Uncle'. I'm addressed as Captain Jennings when I send for you, and you'll keep your place until I do."

Isom whispered to me as we followed the seaman forward to where the bos'n was working. "Marse Jake, how am I going to let my pa know what happened to us?"

"From what that other man said, Captain Jennings sails back and forth between New Orleans and Galveston. I'll try to post a letter to Uncle Harry's wife when we get to New Orleans.

"She'll want to know what happened to her husband and their sons, but I won't mention your father or you. I'll just ask her to let the rest of my relatives know that me and a friend had signed on to Uncle Henry's ship *Eureka*. Your pa will hear and figure it out, and next time we get the chance we'll look for a message on that board outside the customs house. If there's nothing there, we'll leave a message ourselves."

Isom was quiet for a while, then whispered "I never heard you say that before, that I was your friend I mean. I never had a white friend before."

That was a lot to think about, but maybe we were. I'd trusted him and Tom and they'd trusted me, to the point that I felt no unease falling asleep at night, knowing they were keeping watch. I didn't have their experience, but if they ever doubted me I'd seen no sign of it. And hadn't we shared the same hardships? Gone hungry together, shared our food when we had it? Huddled under the same trees to keep from getting soaked?

Friends? Close enough, I figured.

***

Closer than I was to my new messmates for a certainty!

They had made it clear that I was the lowest of the low, a landsman and waister unfit to climb among the bewildering tangle of *lines* that led up the thick masts.

"Not *ropes*, you sorry excuse for a lubber!" the able seaman that had charge of my working party had told me, and I'd believed him. He'd also made it clear that I would never be allowed to climb the ratlines that led dizzyingly to the heights where *real*

25

sailors worked.

Isom had been assigned to a different mess; they slung their hammocks over on the port side, and while some would work the square-rigged mainmast with me and my messmates, most would work the gaff-rigged sails on the mizzen mast aft.

Sailors insisted that they spoke American, but I had my doubts.

I had time as I crawled exhausted into my hammock at the end of my watch to wonder if Isom was as tired as I was, but then sleep claimed me.

Chapter Four

"See that you coat them well, Young Jake, shrouds and ratlines both!" advised Sam Sanford.

I nodded tiredly and dipped the swab into the bucket of hot tar, ensuring that it was well-covered with the smelly stuff. Inevitably, some of the sticky tar wound up on my clothing and on me. I wiped the swab on the upright shrouds, then the ratlines between, pressing hard and then smoothing the new coat so that when the sail-handlers heading aloft put their hands and feet on the lines, they wouldn't slip.

I'd already coated the wooden battens that served the same purpose lower down before moving up. Being allowed to climb higher in the shrouds than my head was a sign that I was gaining confidence, not that I took much pride in that. Far above me, there were more shrouds from the mast-tops that led to the upper masts, connected by ratlines just like the ones I was working on now. That was where the real sailors worked!

Was this how novice sailors gained confidence, by working on the lower stays for a few days as I was doing? Then climbing to the next level during each daylight watch?

Maybe. For now, I was content with my status as 'waister', a lowly landsman who labored in the ship's waist.

Swabbing a fresh coating of tar on lines was one of the easiest jobs on the ship. The rest of the work was hard, but required little thinking. Manning the capstan when the anchor was hoisted, hauling on halyards to align the yards when the wind shifted, re-balancing cargo in the holds as supplies were used up; in each case, the chief requirement was brute strength and endurance.

I'd thought myself inured to hard labor when I joined Eureka's company. Had I not loaded and unloaded packs from mules, wrestled the stubborn beasts to make them stand still while being saddled? All that I had done, and more? Yet I had found during that first week that I was sore in places I didn't know I had! And tired, which soon became a constant state of affairs.

Sleep was something to be caught whenever possible, because the cry of "All hands on deck!" could come at any time and the penalty for not responding fast enough was being turned out without warning from your hammock.

I grew irritable, and I confess, savagely mean. I was easily provoked during that period before I became accustomed to life on board a ship.

My messmates understood, and most avoided me when possible. Others there were who thought to try my readiness to defend myself, and I conducted myself very well in the brief exchanges.

A boy who lives with male cousins learns early how to wrestle, and yes, to fight.

Sam Sanford was my teacher, and strict he was but not overly so.

From learning the names of the standing and running rigging to the location of lines which I had to be able to lay hands on in pitch blackness, to learning of how shrouds supported the masts by connecting to the ship's framing timbers; from knowing how the rudder-lines were rove through pulleys belowdecks and brought up to the wheel, even to reading the compass card in the binnacle; these things he taught me, and more. He was unsparing in praise when I did well and harsh with criticism when I forgot.

I rarely saw Isom, which, according to Sam, was by design. "You must learn to work with your messmates, lad. They must be able to depend on you at all times and in all weathers, and if we sight pirates, well...you'll not be allowed to shirk that duty either!

"The great guns, such as they are," he chuckled, "are fit for wiping away boarders, but of little use else. You'll be called on to help when the time comes, and that smartly, but 'tis easier to handle canister than solid shot." He'd gone on to explain that canister was a tin of musket balls that broke apart during firing, spraying the balls shotgun-like across a pirate's deck. The balls were deadly at close range, worthless beyond a hundred yards.

But the greatest danger *Eureka* would face during the voyage to New Orleans, when all hands might be called out at any time, was not from pirates but from weather.

Late summer in the Gulf was prime hurricane season.

***

Sam, being an able-seaman, often had duties more important than serving as sea-daddy to a raw landsman.

When he was otherwise engaged, I found myself often in the company of Jean-Louis Lafitte, who was about my age. Not so tall as my own 6 foot of height nor as strong as I had become, he was cat-quick and well educated, which I envied.

He was guarded about his forebears, revealing little, yet willingly did he share much other knowledge with me. He helped me improve my writing, something I sorely needed, and later he was outgoing when teaching me to speak French and Spanish.

"When we reach New Orleans, Jake," he said, "you'll be glad you can speak properly!

"The men might be soldiers from Spain or Mexico so you'll need to know Spanish if you're to stay out of trouble, but it's the women who'll appreciate a polite command of French! Otherwise, you'll find yourself restricted to the company of doxies along the waterfront that I'd not wish on my worst enemy!"

So it was that on any given watch, we might spend our time conversing solely in French or Spanish while others sat around in idleness, telling yarns or doing scrimshaw when not needed to work the sails or yards.

Later, Jean-Louis asked permission of the master's mate to begin instructing me in the use of the sword.

That's when I discovered just how quick he was, for I could never touch him. He seemed utterly confident, even bored, when a riposte took my bated-blade out of position, leaving me open to the touch of his bare weapon.

I, the novice, must use a sword with a covered tip; he, the expert, disdained such. And there was more. "Your pistol is fine for one shot, Jake, but you'll have no opportunity to reload in a fight. When that day comes, you'll know the true value of a blade!"

"Did your father teach you, Jean-Louis?" I asked.

"I hardly knew him," he said softly. "He was often away, leaving me in the care of my aunt and her friend Dominique You. From the time when I was barely able to hold an epée in my hand until he went off to fight the British, he taught me. A master not only of blades Dominique was, but of cannon too. He's retired now, or so I was told.

"You'll not see many landsmen wearing a sword openly nowadays, Jake, but don't be fooled. The bravos swagger about with knives patterned on that of James Bowie, but the really dangerous men are armed with pistol and sword-cane."

"I met Jim Bowie once," I recalled. "He's as nice a fellow as you'd ever want to meet. A little stocky of build, quiet, and very good manners, nothing like what you might expect from his reputation. He and my uncle Harry did business together, which is how I came to meet him.

"We brought Texas mustangs from San Augustine across the Sabine to Alexandria, and Jim or his brother Rezin bought them from us. They then sold them to buyers in Mississippi and Alabama. He was engaged to a girl from Alexandria when I met him, but I heard that she died."

"I believe he worked with…a close relative at one time," said Jean-Louis cautiously, "but that was several years ago."

After that, he changed the subject and refused to say more about his early life.

*****

From time to time, I saw Captain Jennings.

I'm sure he knew what I was about, but I was too busy most of the time to concern myself with his doings. If he wanted me, he would send for me.

I saw nothing of New Orleans when we anchored in the river, other than what was visible from *Eureka*'s deck. I had no money, so was not disappointed in not being allowed to go ashore. There would be other opportunities. I did manage to write a letter to my aunt, and when he heard what I was about the captain paid to send it.

Meanwhile, I was kept busy on board, obeying the orders of William Moore, captain of the mainmast.

He seemed pleasant enough during the first few days, but then went ashore and remained there for two days. When he came back, his attitude had changed. My uncle had strict rules about alcohol on board, especially for the hands, but perhaps the rule was different for petty officers. Moore was often either drunk or recovering from the excesses of drink.

Then it was that I learned why his nickname among the crew was "Bully", for in one of his rages he came at me.

The footwork I'd learned from Jean-Louis kept me from serious injury, yet I was unable to avoid many of his punches. I might have suffered a serious beating had the master's mate not seen what was happening and spoken harshly to Moore. Thereafter, I avoided the man and the mate made sure that Moore was watched closely.

Yet he continued to drink, and except for his cronies, other members of the crew showed the marks of his fists.

Two weeks later, we worked our way down the channel at first light and caught the morning ebb tide, which carried us out to the Gulf.

I went aloft for the first time while *Eureka* was underway, only to the lowest yard I confess, but I was no longer among the lowest on board, a mere landsman and waister. I was becoming a sailor.

"One hand for the ship, lad, one hand for yerself! Ye may think me over-cautious, but 'tis a lesson never to be forgotten! One day, when yer hands are bloody and ye're handing a frozen topsail and yer mates are depending on you to take in a reef, all while the main truck is drawing circles above yer head, 'twill save yer life." Old Mario, who'd gone to sea while yet a child, nodded his head and glared at me with his single eye.

I made up my mind to remember his words and practice them whenever I was aloft.

Would I one day do as he'd suggested, join the topmen? Become one of the elite among real sailors, true masters of their craft who thought nothing of going aloft in a gale?

For now, the weather was mild and I soon learned to enjoy the view from high above the deck.

Two weeks later, my heart nearly beating its way out of my chest, I slid down the backstay as real sailors do.

Frightened of falling I was, but more fearful of the mockery that would come if I persisted in my lubberly ways! Jean-Louis was there to steady me when I landed, with a smile and a nod. Perhaps he had been equally—concerned—at one time, and as I had done, faced his fears as a man must and gone on to do what was needed.

***

I was part of the watch on deck when I heard the hail from the crow's nest.

"Deck, thar! Sail ho, two points abaft the larboard bow!"

The sails were drawing well, the breeze steady but not particularly strong from the southeast, and my uncle had been talking to the steersman when he heard the call. Now he walked forward until he was halfway between the foremast and mainmast, then called to the lookout.

"What do you make of her?" he yelled, hands cupped to either side of his mouth that the man aloft might better hear.

"She's Spanish, judging by her rig, and hull-down. I can make out two masts, both full-rigged!"

The master's mate had come up to join my uncle Henry.

"Captain?" he asked. "A pirate, you think?"

"Aye," my uncle said, but he didn't seem worried. "We'll keep an eye on her, but if the breeze holds I expect we're safe enough. I had intended to wait off the channel and go in on the morning tide, but that may change if that fellow comes closer.

"Leave the guns unloaded for now and let the hands rest, but if things change I'll want you to issue weapons."

The mate nodded and went about his business.

As it happened, the pirate turned away to the south, giving up any attempt at a chase. But my uncle was not going to take unnecessary chances.

"We'll anchor in the bay and keep a sharp eye out tonight," he told the mate. "The gunners will have to sleep at their posts. Load the guns before dark, but do not prime them unless ordered. 'Tis best to also have crew weapons ready to hand if needed. I don't anticipate trouble from that fellow, but 'tis best to not take chances."

The mate nodded assent.

"Only a few clouds and we'll have a half-moon tonight," my uncle continued. "If they send boats during the darkness, we'll see them."

After that, the two headed aft, still talking.

Isom came up to me later. "Marse Jake, if anything happens, you'll let my pa know?"

"I will, but you'll be fine. How are things otherwise?"

"I like the work," he said. "Setting and reefing the gaff mainsail is carried out from the deck by halyards, so 'tis easier than what you do. Our tops'l is also smaller than the main tops'l, so my mess has fewer members."

I picked up on the comment about numbers. "No problems?" I asked.

He shrugged, but refused to say more, so I knowed he'd had trouble. Some there were who paid more attention to a man's color than to the quality of his work, but I understood there was no changing them.

After a few more words, he headed back to larboard.

I found a position out of the way, not particularly uncomfortable, but even so I was unable to sleep.

The night passed slowly and I started at every splash from alongside. Eventually the sun came up and revealed that we were alone in the outer bay. So ended my first pirate scare.

The land breeze was foul the next morning, coming directly across the bow, but we were able to tow the ship to a better anchorage. I was assigned to one of the longboat's starboard oars during this task, and looking around I realized my shipmates were as exhausted as I was. But we concentrated on our tasks, as sailors do.

I managed a few hours of sleep during the next watch, while others shifted cargo in preparation for off-loading, then went ashore as part of the longboat's crew. I had no desire to sample such entertainments as there were, and anyway I had received only a partial pay from my uncle.

So it was that I was sitting on a hummock of sand, looking out over the bay at nothing in particular, when Isom found me.

"Marse Jake, I've heard from my pa," he said softly.

"I'm glad, Isom. He got your family out of Louisiana?"

"Aye, he did, but he's had trouble. It's why he's not here now to see you. They must go on, and they'll need my help.

"There was a murder in Natchitoches while my pa was there, of a mulatto freedman who had married a quadroon. Slavers took her and her children west across the Sabine and tried to sell them, but local officials of the Mexican government found out and ordered the men whipped. Because of that and some talk he overheard, Pa thinks it too dangerous for us to stay here.

"Planters are coming to Texas and they'll need slaves to do the work, so as soon as we can collect up supplies and buy a wagon and mules, we're heading west.

"We will go beyond the desert, to where cotton law doesn't hold like it does here in the east. Pa hasn't decided what we'll do when we get there; we might cross the Rio Grande at El Paso del Norte, or we might cross farther north and see about settling around the town of Mesilla. He wants to know what your thoughts are, for you're welcome to come with us. We'll help you get land of your own out there if that's your choice."

But by the time he finished speaking, I knew what I wanted to do.

"I'm staying aboard, Isom. I understand why you have to go, and sorry I am that it has come to this, but my future is with my uncle.

"I won't forget you, any of you. Thank your pa for me when you see him. None of us can be sure about what the future holds, so we may see each other again." I held out my hand and we shook, then ended up hugging each other.

Isom nodded when we stepped apart, likely as choked up as me, and turned away. I watched until he vanished among the sheds and for a short time longer, for it occurred to me that with him went the last of my youth.

Chapter Five

"Mark my words, my boy; keep on as you're going and you'll go far!"

But I barely heard my uncle's words, so anxious was I to share the wondrous news with my best friend Jean-Louis.

"I'm to be the new foremast captain! And my uncle says that next time we sail, he'll start teaching me navigation! I'll need my own sextant, for he'll not risk his fine Dollond instrument that he got from Jean Lafitte, who took it from a British captain. But there are others almost as fine to be had in New Orleans!"

"That's all well and good, Jake, but if you're to be foremast captain, what of Bully Moore?" Jean-Louis asked. "Has your uncle decided to set him ashore?"

"He didn't say. Too many incidents of drinking aboard, too much dissatisfaction among the crew because of his bullying ways, and too many foremast hands leaving the ship at New Orleans were what he mentioned.

"I'm for going ashore where I hope to locate replacement sailors, but I'd admire to buy you a glass of brandy while I look around! What say you?"

"I say yes, and thank you! You will make a fine ship's master one day!"

We took the longboat in with the last of the cargo and beached it near the shed where buyers waited. After seeing to the unloading and storing, which were part of my new responsibilities, we headed for Galveston.

Jean-Louis seemed to be quieter than usual on the way, but I paid little note, such was my mood. Until he put a hand on my sleeve and stopped me, just before we reached the dirt road which was often as far as sailors went into the town, it being the location of grog shops and other places of entertainment.

"Jake, you should watch your back when we return to the ship. Did you mark the look of Smathers and Oakey, who manned the bow oars on our way in? They've had their fiddly businesses going on board, buying a few small things and selling when next we arrive at a port, all watched over by Moore. Now that you're taking his place they'll be wondering, and likely they're not alone for Moore had his favorites. 'Twas his own fault and the captain's decision, but they'll blame you. 'Tis easy enough to cause you to slip when you're aloft and if it happens during the dark of night, who's to know but what your death was an accident?"

"You're right," I said, "and good advice you're giving me, my friend! I'll be careful. I'll also let them know that so long as they don't endanger the ship, they can continue their fiddles to their heart's content!"

As it turned out, the danger was more immediate. We had but stepped into one of the better saloons along the way when Jean-Louis poked my arm. "Moore!" he whispered.

But I had already seen him rising from a table where several other Eureka hands sat. Watched him heading toward us, brushing others away from his path. And just before he got to me, he bellowed, "Take my place, would you, you jumped-up toady?" Before I could respond, I saw the knife in his hand, held low with the blade cutting-edge-up for the gutting stroke.

I pushed Jean-Louis aside, for this was not his affair.

I carried a knife too, as all sailors do, but it was in its sheath on my right hip where I could not reach it in time. I backed up until my hip touched the bar, then placed my hand on top, thinking to vault across if I had time. But my hand fell on the club that the bartender used to start the bungs that sealed his beer tuns.

His carelessness in not placing it in its usual place saved my life, for my hand closed naturally around it.

Not a true bung-starter, it was more of a short club; but it was all I had for I'd no time to reach for my knife. I had time for a brief thought only, that he was a knife fighter and I was not. But the bung-starter was not unlike one of the belaying pins that all sailors handle.

So I swung it at his head as hard as I could.

He saw it coming, and to give him his due, he was uncommonly quick as well as uncommonly strong. He turned his head aside, causing me to miss, but he was no longer balanced to stick his knife in my guts.

Which gave me time to set myself for another swing. I made to aim the bung-starter at his knife wrist but he pulled it back before I could, and with his left hand extended to catch my arm or block the next swing he came at me again.

His knife was near to touching my guts when my next swing connected.

Not where I'd intended, against the side of his head just above the ear, but it staggered him.

He braced his left hand on the bar and spat out teeth and a gobbet of blood, shook his head, then came for me again.

But this time he was slower, and the hard-swung end of the bung-starter struck true. I heard the faint cracking sound as it crushed in the side of his head, and he dropped to the sawdust layer that served for a floor. I looked down, expecting him to rise, but he was dead as the salted beef from *Eureka*'s casks.

Jean-Louis picked up the knife Moore had dropped and examined it, then glanced at the table he had come from.

"Not what I would prefer, but 'twill do, I expect." So saying, he reached for his own knife. I transferred the club to my left hand and drew my knife with my right. If 'twas to be a fight, I was ready.

"Now, lads," Jean-Louis said calmly, "ye have a choice, ye do. Take up his quarrel, or take up his body and see to the disposing of it. What say ye, lads? For I've a thirst that only brandy will quench, and if your choice is to dispose of his body, why, such work makes a man thirsty! I'll buy ye a brandy before you depart, and yer new foremast captain will buy the next. What say ye, lads?"

They took the brandy, though more than one had already taken aboard more drink than he should, then dragged Moore's body outside.

Only then did Jean-Louis sigh with relief and put his knife

away.

Moore's he stuck in the bar and slammed his hand against the handle's side, breaking the blade. "A cheap thing, but dangerous," he remarked, looking at the bar-tender where he waited down the bar. "You can leave your place and the shotgun that's behind you, for the trouble is over. We'll have another brandy each, the best you have this time, and my friend will pay for them."

The barman nodded, found a dusty bottle behind the bar that stood apart from the cheaper stuff he'd sold us earlier, and poured two glasses full.

The quiet that had fallen while the fight was in progress vanished as sailors at other tables talked about what they'd seen.

"We'll have to leave the ship, you know," Jean-Louis said softly.

I nodded, for I understood. There would be resentment at the very least, possibly more.

Jean-Louis had spoken truly; there were many opportunities aboard ship to do away with a man, and I could not do my work and protect myself as well. And because he'd stood by me, his time on board was ending too.

A last trip out to *Eureka* we made, to explain what had happened to my uncle, and collect any pay that was due us.

He selected a crew of trusted hands to ferry us ashore in the smaller gig, and this time when we turned away I knew we had seen the last of her.

***

We sought temporary lodgings in Galveston and looked about before finding a place to eat.

Red snapper was the choice offered and a fine one it was, for it came properly cooked with rice and with beans alongside. The coffee tasted fine as well, especially so as there was none to be had aboard *Eureka*. We had a second cup apiece, along with a slice of cobbler thick with blackberries, and talked about what we should do now.

"We shall need work," I said, for I'd little to show for my two years afloat after paying for our meal.

He nodded agreement. "There are labor jobs, but there's no

future in them. I do not regret leaving *Eureka*, for I have been thinking for some time that I should leave the sea. Too many hear my name and wonder if I'm the son or grandson of Jean Lafitte the pirate."

I thought to ask him if it was true, but I remembered that he had never seemed willing to talk of his past and changed the topic.

"There's land to be had, if you're willing to become Mexican," I pointed out. "I care not which church claims me, and as for the language, we both speak Spanish. You are as fluent as any Mexican and I can speak it passably well, so we should be able to find work."

"I know little of farming or ranching," Jean-Louis confessed. "Most of what I know has to do with ships and the sea. I would not wish to join the Mexican Army, although I believe I could serve well should it come to that."

"It won't," I replied. "I have been a farmer. I've also trapped and fished, and I know about handling mules and caring for a team. As you taught me, so shall I teach you! But first, we must have money for a wagon, tools, mules or oxen, and other things we need. It may be that one of the entrepreneurs who bring in new settlers will offer us work. It does no harm to ask, and while we work for him we'll learn what we must know."

Ask we did, but none there were in Galveston. Yet the idea of learning while doing would not go away.

Jean-Louis found work with the master of an ox-drawn wagon train as a general helper. By the time they reached their destination at Bexar, he was certain that he would have learned much that would be helpful to us later. But the train had work for only one, as was also the case with the man I hired out to. Jean-Louis and me separated, promising to meet later on when we had the chance.

***

Noah Smithwick, his name was, and he was already a seasoned immigrant with a trade, a shop, and more work than he could handle alone.

So I pumped the bellows, hauled the iron bars into the smithy when needed, shouldered the hundred-pound bags of coal that fed the forge, and did such other work as he found for me. A week later, he showed me how to shoe a horse and supervised while I did the next one myself.

I rasped down the hooves, using a tool that Noah made, shaped the hot shoe to fit, then nailed it carefully into place, ensuring that the nail came out the side of the hoof in position for clinching. A farrier can cripple a horse by a nail turned the wrong way, but I was careful and Noah never had cause to regret hiring me.

Two months later, after I had become expert at caring for hooves, he began teaching me the trade of blacksmithing.

I started out by making tools, not only rasps and files, but the more complicated tongs and hammers. I shaped them and punched the holes with care. Tongs where the jaws don't close properly is useless, and a hammer handle that's in the right place is easy and a joy to use. An unbalanced tool will leave you exhausted.

Our customers saw no need to complain about my work. I never approached Noah's artistry, but my tongs were soon as functional as any and I could temper wrought iron as well as he. For he had already looked on too many glowing pieces fresh from the forge, a thing that would one day take his sight.

But neither of us knew that at the time, and for myself, I was happy just to approach his level of skill in that one way if no other. Gradually, I took over the blacksmithing, leaving Noah to concentrate on repairing firearms. He'd learned the associated trade of gunsmith during his apprenticeship, and on the frontier a gunsmith will never want for work.

***

This arrangement continued for more than a year and I was content enough, except that no smith likes the feel of hot cinders blistering his forearms. But the leather sleeves to my vest had to be put aside in summer, for heat and humidity in a smithy can kill.

Like others before me had done, I brushed off the tiny bits of hot slag and worked on.

We were busy for the most part, but one day I picked up a Pennsylvania rifle that Noah had repaired. I admired it and thought back to my cousin's prized rifle; could this be the same one?

There was no way to tell. They were as alike as two peas from the same pod.

Noah saw the envy on my face and remarked that it was time I learned gunsmithing. "Starting tomorrow, Jake, when you've a spare few minutes, you'll begin making a rifle for yourself. A man who can build his own from raw wood and iron is a man who can repair any that will come into his shop!"

Chapter Six

I worked steadily on my rifle when time permitted, but made sure not to neglect my smithing and farrier work. Noah occasionally checked my work to ensure that my standards were as high as his own.

He also looked at the progress I was making on the rifle, and finally asked what I thought I was doing. He brought over his Pennsylvania long rifle so that I could compare my work with his, and to explain why he didn't like mine.

"You're making a *cannon*, Jake! My rifle is .40 caliber, yours looks to be a full half inch across at the muzzle! And that stock you're building! It's *walnut*, not curly maple!"

"Mine is designed more like the Hawken," I explained. "It's .54 caliber and the barrel is shorter, but still accurate, and unlike yours, mine will fetch a buffalo when I'm done with it. I also plan on using iron furnishings instead of brass. I'll grant that yours *looks* better, but when I'm done I expect mine will *shoot* better!"

That set the cat among the mockingbirds for fair!

Noah wouldn't speak to me for three days, and after that it was mostly about business.

I was grateful for all he'd taught, but a man has to go his own way at some point and I was stubborn enough to figure I had the right of things.

Time to time after that, I heard Noah out back, banging away with his rifle. Practicing, I figured. I grinned and kept on working.

His rifle had a regular single-trigger lock, but mine would have the newer set-triggers. A body could shoot in a hurry by a hard pull on that front trigger, but if he had time, squeezing the rear trigger set up the front one to fire the piece if a fellow breathed hard on it!

A Pennsylvania-style trigger was easier to make, but if the Hawken brothers could make set-triggers, I reckoned I could too. It helped that I had taken one of their rifles with a ruined barrel in trade. I took that rifle apart and studied all the lock parts before starting on mine.

The tapered octagonal barrel blank was easy enough to forge and cutting the grooves for the rifling was simple, even though it took work to get it right. I spent as much time scraping out those rifling grooves as I had forging the barrel blank itself! Making the percussion lock with its complicated sear, ratchet, pawl, and springs also took time, but I got it done. Hot-filing small parts is fussy work!

The next step was to rough-in the half-stock and inlet it to hold the barrel, lock, and triggers where they were supposed to be. When I was satisfied with the fit, I carved a beavertail cheek rest on the stock.

It was starting to look like a rifle, but there was more to be done.

Before doing the final smoothing, I chiseled out two mortises, one near the butt for patches, a smaller one in front that would hold two dozen percussion caps. Unlike flints for the older-style locks, I wouldn't be able to make new caps if I ran out.

The raw wood I finished with a mixture of beeswax dissolved in hot tallow and the iron furnishings were browned like the barrel and lock.

I had made friends among the townspeople, doing a favor now and then when help was needed. So it was that my chickens showed up to roost just before my rifle was finished; one of the men I'd helped to build a cabin made me a scrimshawed powder horn, and a widow in a different way sewed me a calfskin possibles-bag for the shot-mold and other things I would need.

One day, when I knowed that she was short of food for her son and two daughters, I'd taken a musket I'd just repaired out to the woods and killed a pig. She had tears in her eyes when I showed up with the meat and insisted on cooking up a proper meal for me. I enjoyed the meal, and when she asked me to stay on for breakfast, I was happy to oblige.

Nice lady; she got married three weeks later to a man who'd

lost his wife to a fever. I made new hinges for her cabin door, the old ones having rusted, and gave them to the couple as a wedding present. He moved in with her and folks later on allowed that he didn't waste much time, their baby boy arriving a tad earlier than expected.

***

Her husband set up shop as a wheelwright and when he needed tires for a set of new wheels, we went down to a wrecked ship that had been driven inland during a storm. Five miles from the sea it was, and the wood had rotted away except for the pitch-pine stumps of the masts. The iron we salvaged was rusty, but usable after I reworked it, and it served well as tires for the Alcalde's new buggy.

The next day, I finished my rifle.

I aligned the sights, shot it a few times, and tapped on the dovetailed sight a bit until it shot true. But Noah didn't seem interested in a shoot-off, despite the practicing he'd done, so I let the matter drop.

A week later, Jean-Louis got back to town. He came by to say howdy and we talked about where he'd been.

"I tell you, Jake, fortunes are being made out there! We already speak Spanish, so all we would have to do is swear to become Catholics and register with the nearest alcalde! As soon as we do that, we can take up land for ourselves, but we need to do it before it's all claimed by Germans!"

"Germans?" I asked.

"Yep, Germans. One or two came in with Steven Austin and since then, there have been more! They're coming in by the *shipload*, way I hear it, because the Mexican government likes having them here. They figure that they're less troublesome than Americans!"

So that afternoon, we looked up the alcalde, told him in Spanish what we had in mind, and walked away as Mexican citizens.

Noah had made up his mind to move west too, so when I told him I was leaving we went our separate ways as friends. He headed north to where Steven F. Austin had settled, and we got ready for our own move. Some of what I'd need to set up as a blacksmith I already owned, the rest I'd bought from him. We loaded it into our new-bought wagon and the next morning, hitched up our team.

We headed northwest, planning to strike the westbound road toward the town of Gonzales that had been rebuilt southeast of San Antonio de Bexar. The original town had been abandoned after two Indian attacks, not that it was much of a town to start with the way I heard the story. The new one was a mile or so south, on the Guadalupe River where the San Marcos flowed in.

The Old San Antonio Road, it was called, although it was more trail than road. Before that it had been the Camino Real, a way for Spaniards to start out from the Rio Grande, pass through San Antonio de Bexar and parallel the coast all the way to Nacogdoches. East of there, it crossed the Sabine river and went on to Natchitoches in Louisiana.

Here and there, trails branched off. Wagon trains followed the road, carrying supplies to the missions and when they came to a cutoff, one or two wagons would turn off and head to the mission.

Most were also fortified presidios that housed a few soldiers. More'n likely, the soldiers who had killed my uncle and cousins had come from one. The missions were having a hard time of it, what with hostile Indians stealing their stock and protestants sneaking across the border. My uncle and cousins had done a fair amount of the sneaking until that Mexican patrol caught up with us, though religion played no part in what we were doing.

***

Jean-Louis added more details as we rolled westward behind our team of mules.

"The Guadalupe River country has only a few settlers right now, but more will come. The government intends to dredge the sandbanks along the lower river and as soon as they do, ships will start bringing in cargoes. They'll need people that know about ships to guide the first ones in, people like us.

"There's already a sizable town on the river at Victoria. De León's colony got there back in 1824 so the best land has been claimed, but Gonzales is still only about two years old. I figure we look around, pick out good land with river access, and take up claims like we talked about doing before. You can set up a smithy and gun-repair shop in the town if you're a mind to, and I'll file a claim and start rounding up mustangs. Your shop will bring in money until our horse business starts paying off."

"My uncle traded in wild horses at one time," I said. "It was part of his two-way trade, smuggle in liquor, tobacco, and coffee from Louisiana and take part of his payment in horses. As I remember, he never had trouble selling them."

"And we won't either! All those new immigrants will need mounts, pack horses, and teams! I tell you, we can make our fortune!"

"You know how to break a horse to saddle?" My skepticism showed. "For I tell you straight, I do not."

"Every horse you see being worked had to be broken before it could be used!" insisted Jean-Louis. "I figure we hire somebody who knows the way of it to start with, then eventually do the work ourselves.

"We'll need to watch out for Indians, though. The Comanches are generally friendly, but they're horse Indians and lazy, the Lipan-Apaches and Kiowas too. They'd rather steal one from us that's already been broke than catch wild ones and do their own breaking!"

"Sounds like it might work," I admitted cautiously. "Hiring someone, that's where I come in, for he'll expect to be paid.

"But if I'm to have a smithy, it will have to be in town like you said, either Gonzales or Victoria. I have a basic set of tools, but I'll need leather for a bellows and rocks to build a forge."

Jean-Louis had no idea of how much work was involved in setting up a proper shop before the first shoe was made and horse shod! So I told him as we rolled along. Talking about our future was pleasant and it kept us busy as the miles rolled by.

I shot an antelope later that afternoon.

Jean-Louis was impressed, and the truth of the matter was that I impressed myself. We paced off the distance to where he lay, almost 400 long paces. That .54 caliber ball had gone through his shoulder and killed him stone dead. We roasted as much as we could comfortably eat, then drove on until just before sundown.

Jean-Louis spotted a promising campsite ahead, atop a wooded knoll where we had a good view of the trail to the south and open woodlands to the north. We'd heard nothing of recent trouble with Indians, but they were apt to be where a body least expected so we took turns guarding our stock that night.

Next morning, we roasted more of the antelope and parched some of our corn. The mules had grazed well during the night, but we put a little of the corn in their nosebags to add a bit of spring to their steps. They chased down every last kernel while we buckled on their harness and had a final cup of coffee apiece.

A man needs to be watchful about feeding corn to his stock. A little is good, but too much puts more spring in than he wants and it don't take much to change a mule from ornery to downright feisty!

A large freight wagon was passing on the road when we drove down from the knoll, so we fell in behind, far enough back to be out of most of the dust but close enough that we could help each other out if there should be trouble.

It wasn't long before two men came galloping back from the wagon to find out our intentions, and after we told them who we were and where we were going, they invited us to camp with them when they stopped for the night.

So we did, a big party being safer than two men traveling alone.

They provided potatoes, beans, and coffee for our evening meal, we contributed the rest of the antelope.

After eating, we settled around the fire and told a few yarns, except for the two men out in the dark keeping watch on the livestock. Afterward, Jean-Louis took a shift with one of the men and I took his place around midnight.

Breakfast was bacon and camp bread, wrapped around a ramrod and baked in the coals while a few of us harnessed our teams. Soon enough, they were back on the road and we were following, but once again far enough behind to avoid most of their dust.

Not that the breeze cooperated, being apt to switch directions nearly as soon as we reached a bend in the road. But we managed, and as game was plentiful within sight of the road, one of the freighters shot a brace of turkeys for our supper.

Four days later we pulled into Gonzales town.

***

The best place to hear the latest information is where whiskey is being sold, so after turning our mules into a public corral and providing them with hay and fresh water we walked into the town.

Houses spread along the east bank of the Guadalupe, most of them two log cabins joined by a covered opening between wide enough for a wagon to pass.

The log walls were thick and chinked; no effort had been made to hew them square. They might be that way because no one in the town possessed an adze or broad-axe that was needed to properly square a log, although a common felling axe could serve if a man knew the way of it. But I owned all three and as soon as my smithy was set up, I could make more.

Doors and window shutters were also thick, made of planks riven from sections of tree trunks. I judged that they would stop any arrow and most bullets. They also had loopholes; the folks that built the houses knowed they might have to fight off Indians, so they made ready ahead of need.

The saloon was one of the larger buildings in town and since the shutters were open, cool inside. I welcomed it after the heat and dust of the trail and I reckon Jean-Louis did too. We drank a glass of beer apiece, which we hadn't tasted for some time, and listened to the conversations.

We'd been there less than ten minutes when I spotted a man I thought I recognized. I motioned the barkeep over and asked, "Is that Jim Bowie?"

"Who wants to know?" His tone was a mite unfriendly, I thought, seeing as we were paying customers.

"I met him several years ago over in Louisiana. Alexandria, it was, and if it's him I figure to go over and say howdy."

"It's Jim, although you might want to be careful. He's been

drinking."

"He's not dressed the way I remember him," I said thoughtfully. "Back then, Jim Bowie was always well-dressed and mannerly."

"Jim's had a rough time of it," the bar-man said. "Lost his wife and children to the cholera, her parents and brother too. He ain't got over it, and some think he never will, but I reckon it would be okay to go over and buy him a drink."

So I did.

He remembered me and seemed glad to see me again. I introduced Jean-Louis, and Jim introduced us to the people he'd been talking to, Edward Burleson and John Moore. They had come to town on business, Jim said. He didn't explain further and I knew better than to ask. If a man wants to tell you his business, he will.

Both were interested in my plan to open a smithy and gunsmith shop, and willingly gave advice. They also had suggestions for where Jean-Louis might find the kind of land he was looking for and promised to introduce him to the alcalde after he found it.

An introduction would be helpful, because Gonzales was the farthest western point that Americans had settled and the closest town of size to San Antonio de Bexar. Mexican officials this far out were suspicious of people who'd come from the United States, and cautious about approving new land grants for them. Jim allowed that it would help that we were already Mexican.

After heading back to the stable where we proposed to bed down close to our mules, Jean-Louis looked at me. "That Moore hombre," he said. "You don't reckon he's kin to the one you killed back in Galveston, do you?"

"Well, I hope not. Fairly common name, I'd say."

"Jake, you watch yourself around him. It's like you said, Moore's a common name and so is Jennings, but there ain't all that many people in Texas and lots are related. I wouldn't rule it out, was I you."

Good advice, I thought, just before sleep took me.

Chapter Seven

I staked out a location on the north edge of Gonzales and started work. People showed up to say howdy and stayed to help.

By the end of that first day we had pulled weeds, dug out bushes, leveled the ground, sprinkled it with a little water, and tramped it solid. That's all the floor a blacksmith needs, unless he expects to burn down his smithy before he gets well started!

The gunsmith's shop next to it would be like most of the other buildings, two log cabins joined by a covered opening between. I figured to live in one and use the other for work.

The space behind the smithy I left for later. After I fenced it in for a corral, which I would need for holding horses and mules while they were waiting to be shod, the animals would take care of clearing out the grass and weeds. What they wouldn't eat, they'd stomp flat in no time.

While we were working, Jean-Louis and a freedman named Joe unloaded our wagon and went hunting. There was game in plenty to be had, folks said, although a body needed to ride an hour or two out of town to find it. Joe knowed where there were good hunting spots closer than that.

He was as good as folks claimed; him and Jean-Louis brought back two does, three turkeys, and a wild sheep of some kind, all field-dressed and skinned. They'd kept one of the deerskins aside to wrap the livers and hearts in; the others they laid hair-side-down on the wagon bed to put the meat on.

I'd never seen the likes of that sheep! Mostly brown he was, with a light-colored rump and big curling horns. He was chunky too, compared with the deer, having as much meat on him as both of those does together! Although, to be fair, the does were a mite on the small side and hadn't regained the weight they'd lost before they got around to weaning their fawns.

People came by the next morning to help, as neighbors do, and the meat was welcome. Several women showed up to do the cooking and most brought more food, including cornbread, a pot of Mexican beans, and four kinds of pie!

I managed to sample all four, and they were right tasty. Too bad those women were married; good as they fed us, I might have thought twice about remaining a bachelor!

The walls, of well-seasoned unhewn logs, werc up by the end of the day. It was understood that when we had time, Jean-Louis and I would head out and help cut trees to replace the ones we'd used.

I found out later they'd been intended for a palisade, but the town had grown so fast that people kept putting the job off, and finally they decided they didn't need a wall around the town after all.

The following day, Jean-Louis and two helpers went off to look at the land that Edward Burleson had recommended, while I joined the fireplace-building crew.

I wondered why they built them in corners instead of in the middle of the wall, but they explained that it was the Mexican way. And since they were Mexican, I figured they knowed what they were doing.

As for me, I was glad someone did!

That afternoon, they hauled rocks and mixed more mud for mortar while I stacked them for my forge, with a hollowed-out space below the firepit for an air pipe. The tuyere I installed was one that I'd brought with me from Galveston, of thick bronze with holes designed to let the air pass but keep small pieces of charcoal and clinker from falling through. Below that was the opening for removing ashes.

Not a real forge yet because I hadn't made a bellows, but it was farther along than I would have expected after only two days of work!

The anvil, nothing more than a large square block of iron, was the one that I'd used in Galveston while learning the trade. Maybe one day I would have a *real* one, with a horn, cutting bench, and hardened face that had hardy and pritchel holes.

Someday…

My hammers and tongs I brought under the roof to protect them, for the clouds had begun rolling up from the south and my helpers needed to get home to see to their own affairs. The post-vise I put aside until I had time to construct a workbench.

***

Over the next few days, I loaned out my spade, froe, felling axe, adze, and broadaxe to the ones who'd helped me.

Some of the borrowers might *not* have helped yet, but they would later. Meantime, they would have smoothed logs to sit on and riven planks for their roofs. Loaning out tools to those who had none didn't harm me. I could always fix something if it broke, and if needed, I could make new. Such was the way of the frontier. Neighbor helped neighbor and when necessary, risked everything, including his life.

The summer passed, and it seemed like there weren't enough hours in the day. Jean-Louis and I worked from first light to deep dusk before falling exhausted into our beds. There were times we were just too tired even to eat. But by the end of August, I had a shop and a growing business, and Jean-Louis had a house and corrals on the 4,428-acre league of land he'd claimed. That's how the Spaniards had reckoned land area, by the league and the 177-acre labor. The Mexicans had just kept the old system when they booted the Spaniards out.

His house was like the one we'd built in Gonzales, but bigger.

The log cabins had window openings with thick shutters that faced out on a covered but unfloored porch, and were connected by a roofed opening wide enough and tall enough to park a wagon. Behind one of the cabins was the cook-space and a ways behind the other was the outhouse.

Families generally lived in one cabin and used the other for a kitchen, but during hot Texas summers most cooked outside. All that was needed was an adobe horno, which is what Mexicans called their ovens, and a firepit with a tripod. At the top was a hook to hang the grate from, and raising or lowering the chain by a link or two was how folks adjusted cooking heat.

Jean-Louis and his crew had also built a wooden landing, not quite a dock, that stuck out into the Guadalupe river, making it easy to draw a bucketful to water the stock. Later on, he figured to put in a pump and a flue to carry water directly to the corrals.

The holding corral and breaking pens were also done, but building a barn would have to wait.

***

While I was busy in Gonzales shoeing horses and repairing guns that should have been replaced, Jean-Louis and two helpers rounded up two dozen mustangs. The best, mostly young, they trained as riding stock, the others were broke to work as draft animals.

Breaking a horse to the saddle was a simple, if difficult, job best done by two men, but teaching horses to draw a plow or a wagon was easier. Just hitch one or two to a stone-boat, which was really no more than a heavy sled with thick hewn-log runners, and let the horses tire themselves out trying to run away from it. We would need teams for our own use, but as soon as the others were ready they would be sold. Most who lived in town had no need for a saddle-mount, but whether oxen, horses, or mules, there was always a market for draft animals.

Others had started with more than we had, but for two who were pulling ourselves up by our own boot-straps we were doing well.

Our neighbors had taken note. Men who will work hard without complaining soon gain the respect of others.

Edward Burleson came by now and then, but John Henry Moore was often in my shop when he visited Gonzales.

I figured that sometimes he was there just to visit, other times he seemed more interested in the repair work I was doing. "That's a nice rifle," he said one day, looking at the one I'd made for myself where it hung on the pegs. "Plains pattern, I take it?"

I nodded. "I made that one. Noah Smithwick was the master smith I worked for, and to be honest, he didn't like it all that much, being that it was patterned on the Hawken. The one he'd made for himself was more like the German-style Pennsylvania rifle, with a longer barrel and more drop at the heel of the stock. I reckoned some of that was because the old flintlocks had a pan that flared up and smoked, so people wanted their faces farther back. Caplocks don't have that problem"

"You'll sometimes get a little smoke coming through the nipple on yours, even though the copper skirt on the cap creates a good seal," John observed, "but I'd call that first-rate work. How does it shoot?"

"Tolerably well. I've killed game out to more than 400 paces, but I reckon .54 caliber to be on the light side for grizzly unless there's a tree to hand."

He grinned at me and confessed that he never wanted to face a wounded silvertip, tree or no, then asked about the kind of work I'd been doing since I opened my shop.

"Now and then I'll need to forge a new hammer or weld one back together," I said, "and you'd be surprised how many trigger guards get lost through carelessness, but most of what I do is make new springs to replace busted ones. Seems like they work-harden over time, even the best-made ones, and there ain't no repairing them. I make my new ones from thin steel that I've already quenched in warm tallow and tempered.

"Quenching in water or brine leaves them too hard, apt to shatter in use, and of course drawing the temper from thin stock ain't easy. It's why there are lot of blacksmiths around but only a few gunsmiths."

"You know your trade," he said. We talked a while longer, then shook hands before he went on his way.

Nary a mention of that other Moore that I'd had difficulty with, which suited me. Maybe they weren't kin after all.

***

Early in September Moore stopped by for a different reason.

"What do you know of happenings down in Mexico?" he asked.

"I hear Santa Anna has took over down there. There was talk about the Constitution of 1824 too, that it had been suspended. There's been fighting here and there since that happened, but I don't reckon it amounts to much."

"It might," he said grimly. "Ed Burleson has been away on a

55

trip to the east, talking to people, and neither one of us likes what we're hearing. I wanted to ask you straight up: if it comes to a fight, how will you stand?"

I didn't need to even think about that one. "With my neighbors, the people that have helped me. I reckon I speak for Jean-Louis too."

He nodded, so I went on, thinking my way along as I did. "Mexico City is a long way from here and I don't see them doing much to help us. The only thing standing between the Indians and us is our own militia.

"I heard talk back in Galveston, that settlers there liked Santa Anna when he was a brigadier general, but I ain't heard nothing good of him lately."

"You're not likely to," he said. "I'll call on you if we've need of your help. Have you ever worked on a cannon?"

"I learned how to load and fire one, but that's all," I admitted. "I didn't know you had one."

"I don't, but the town has two that Mexico loaned us in case the Indians attacked in force. I'd like you to take a look at them, especially the big one."

So I did.

The bronze six-pounder barrel looked solid, but the touch-hole had been plugged at some time, then drilled out. Either the one who'd drilled it had used a bit that was too large, or it had eroded during firing since then, meaning a lot of the explosion would blow out through the touch-hole. It would make a lot of noise, but how far would it cast a cannonball?

Not far, I reckoned.

The wooden undercarriage was cracked in places and the straps holding the barrel to the wooden support were rusty. But after I took a closer look, I decided they would serve. All in all, despite the cracks in the wood, it was better than one I'd heard about back east.

The owner had a half-pounder esmeril that he intended to use against Indians who had stolen his horses. He'd strapped it to a jackass's back and headed off to find the Indians. He had no carriage, but he decided that wouldn't be a problem; just load it and shoot from the jackass's back!

Getting the jackass turned around so that the barrel was aimed took some doing, but finally he decided the aim was good enough and touched it off. Using a jackass to *transport* a cannon was one thing; shooting it from off the animal's back was different.

The poor creature had turned a somersault in the air and shed that cannon as soon as he could by scraping it off against a tree.

Noah, who told me the story, was sure it had happened, but I had my doubts. I've handled jackasses a time or two and getting them to stand in one place long enough to aim anything stronger than a fart?

Naw.

***

Gonzales Town had another, smaller cannon, a one-pounder esmeril with an iron barrel, so I worked it over to make sure it would serve if needed. But my shop was too cramped to do anything with the six-pounder, what with my gunsmithing tools and bench taking up a lot of the room, so I walked down to my neighbor John Sowell's shop and talked to him.

"Might be that the best way to fix that carriage is to use what we've already got," he said thoughtfully. "A pair of wheels off of Albert Martin's cotton wagon ought to serve, so if you'll give me a hand, I 'spect we'll get it done."

John Moore stopped by with several men after we told him the job was finished. He seemed satisfied, so I reckon we were too. The men took the cannons away and I thought no more of the matter.

Mexico likely had a lot more cannons, better ones too, and Gonzales wasn't much of a town to start with. If there was to be trouble, it would fall on a big place like Galveston, where ships could bring in an army and land it onshore.

Or if he didn't care to take a sea trip, Santa Anna could just march his soldiers north to Bexar. He might also choose to turn right and pass through Goliad on the way to Galveston.

But I wouldn't want to haul supplies for an army over any Texas road I'd seen. Rations, fodder for the animals, powder and shot…it would take another army just to keep the first one fed! Turned out I was somewhat pessimistic.

Chapter Eight

Summer was coming to a close.

Along the Guadalupe, wild sunflowers were in full bloom, their yellow petals attracting birds and other wildlife. Persimmons were ripe and the walnuts, hickory-nuts, and pecans would soon be dropping.

Seemed like every day somebody came in with wild fruits or nuts and maybe a comb of honey from a bee tree they'd raided, wanting me to take it in trade for fixing up an old gun. Most of them I would have either left lay where they were found or maybe hung up on deer antlers as decorations; but if they wanted them fixed, I said I would as soon as I got time.

Not all were that bad; two converted percussion rifles came in, one with a cracked stock, the other with a badly shattered fore-end. I looked at Dave, who owned the rifle, and he looked ashamed but finally explained. "I shot a deer and he looked plumb dead until I was ready to field-dress him. I had my knife in my right hand and my rifle in my left, not wishing to leave it more than a step away while I was working. More than one hombre has lost his hair by doing that!

"Anyway, I was about to lay my rifle against a beech tree when that deer woke up. Danged if he didn't look right unhappy with me, and since he had a full rack of antlers and I had no wish to face them with a knife, I dropped it and whacked him across the head with my rifle. I only needed one lick, which I reckon was just as well. You reckon you can fix it?"

"Nope. But I can carve you out a new stock at least as good as that one. What happened to the deer?"

"I fetched him, of course," Dave said. "Want one of the backstraps? Mighty tasty they are!"

I shared the backstrap with Jean-Louis, who'd come to town to hear voices that weren't the same ones he heard every day. After we ate, we headed over to the saloon, which wasn't all that refined, but did have cool beer for them that wanted it and coffee for the ones that didn't.

The barkeep had whiskey too, or said that's what it was. But one man claimed he'd seen him throw a rattlesnake in the barrel to give his whiskey more kick. The barkeep didn't actually *deny* it, but said that the only rattler he'd seen recently had been small.

We were standing at the bar and drinking our beers, catching up on what we'd been doing since Jean-Louis' last visit, when John Moore walked in. He headed straight for us and Jean-Louis looked a trifle concerned for a moment, but I said howdy to John and offered to buy him a beer if he wished to join us.

"I'd like to, Jake, but I've got no time right now. Looks like the whole Mexican Army is here!"

I blinked at that and looked at Jean-Louis, who shrugged his shoulders. "I didn't notice a dust cloud when I came in to town. Can't be very many of them."

"Old Laban might have fudged the numbers a mite," John said, "but they're soldiers, right enough. The good thing is that they're on the other side of the Guadalupe and they'll not be able to cross until the water level goes down. I reckon that will be about a week from now, unless it rains more between now and then."

"You want us to join you?" I asked. "I 'spect I could shoot across the river and do for one or two before they could find a tree to hide behind."

"Not right now," John said. "I've already got eighteen volunteers keeping an eye on them. Not enough to stop them from crossing, at least not yet. But I've sent riders to notify other militia companies and if they get here before the river goes down, I'll have enough to chase that bunch back to Mexico with their tails between their legs!

"Some of the volunteers are poorly armed, and when I found that out I thought of you. Do you have rifles, or at least muskets, that we could borrow? They'd have to be usable, mind you."

"I've got some, but they don't belong to me. I don't know as how I ought to just hand them over without talking to their owners," I told him.

"What if I guaranteed that you'll get them back, or if they're lost I'll make it right with the owners myself? I wouldn't ask if I didn't need them," John said.

"Let's go," I said.

We drank down the last of our beer, Jean-Louis and me, and headed for the shop. I had a few rifles there that I had been working on, and two old muskets I thought were safe enough if not overcharged with powder. Several other men came in right behind us and John saw to passing the rifles out. The muskets he refused, and I can't say I blamed him.

"What about those two?" He pointed to the two on pegs behind my bench, waiting for me to carve new stocks to replace the broken ones. I explained that one was cracked behind the lock, where the stock is smaller, and the other was the one that had killed a deer by clubbing.

I didn't explain how it happened, because I had my doubts. Buck fever, with maybe a cargo of whiskey on board to make that deer look like a giant with a bigger rack than a longhorn steer?

He examined the two. "They'll do. You've got rawhide, I'm sure. Use it."

I understood what he wanted right away, and nodded. Not a permanent fix, but it would serve for one fight at least.

"How are you fixed for horses?" Jean-Louis asked.

"Not nearly as many as I'd like. The Mexicans are dragoons; they usually travel on horseback, dismount after they arrive, and then fight as infantry. But if they stay mounted, I don't have enough horses for my volunteers to chase them off."

"I've got about twenty I can loan you, if your men are good riders," Jean-Louis offered. "They're apt to buck of a morning, especially if the night was cold."

"I'll take them," John said, "and you have my gratitude for offering. Shall I count on you two to stand with us when the fighting commences?"

We agreed that we would, and after shaking our hands, John went off to see to other tasks.

Jean-Louis headed for the ranch to round up the horses and I set to work cutting the rawhide thongs I would soak and wrap around the broken stocks. They would shrink as they dried, and with a coating of beeswax to keep out the damp, they would do well as temporary fixes. I'd seen a number with such wraps, some that looked to be several years old, so maybe 'temporary' wasn't the right description.

John hadn't mentioned it, but our untried militia had up to now done no more than frighten off Indian boys intending to steal horses.

Could they stand up to professional Mexican soldiers? They would try, meaning there would be spare weapons aplenty after the fighting ended.

If the men who needed them were still in condition to fight.

***

I acquitted myself well the next morning, despite not having done much riding in recent months. I stayed on the horse, despite his objections, and there were some who got to practice mounting several times before we were ready to head out. But nothing much happened during that day, other than men trickling in from other settlements. Our numbers swelled until I estimated that along with our visitors, who soon outnumbered the locals, we had more men under arms than that Mexican lieutenant did.

And everyone was anxious for the fighting to commence, except for me. I had *seen* what Mexican troops could do. How many of our eager volunteers could say as much? But a man does not betray his neighbors if he is to call himself a man, and besides, I had given John Moore my word. I had little else of value, but I treasured my honor as men of wealth and position often do not.

I would stand with my fellow Texians, come what may.

***

The Guadalupe's water level continued to fall, but our numbers kept on growing as it did. I figured the Mexicans would soon try to cross the river, but most would never come out when they did.

As it happened, they didn't. Lieutenant Castañeda, the

commander of the Mexican force, had spies watching us just like we had spies watching them, and they reported the increase in our numbers. Not only did we now have more men than he did, we had those two cannons ready to shred his troops with musket balls as soon as they entered the water.

Late that afternoon, the Mexicans quietly packed up and abandoned their camp. But they didn't do what we expected, head back toward San Antonio de Bexar. They turned upriver and kept going for about seven miles, then set up a new camp.

John Moore met for some time with his lieutenants, listening to what they had to say, then ordered us to cross the river and follow them, but quietly.

We stopped right after they did, about two hours after we'd started. While they set up a regular Mexican Army camp, Jean-Louis and I shared our jerky with some who had not been so foresighted before bedding down to sleep if we could.

I did sleep, although not well. Several times during that long night I sat up, listening for the sounds of fighting that never came. And each time, despite the warmth of my blankets, I had a difficult time getting back to sleep.

***

The moon was low in the sky next morning when one of the camp guards came around to wake us. Quietly he informed us to prepare, for John Moore had made up his mind to force a battle as soon as it was light enough to tell friend from foe.

I saddled my horse, not quite so corral-sour today as he'd been the day before, and by feel checked that the cap was still in place over my rifle's nipple.

It was.

I would have drawn the old charge and reloaded, but doing so in the dark, not knowing when we would be ordered to charge the Mexicans? *Too risky*, I thought, and between the seal created by the percussion cap and the wadding over the ball, my powder *should* be dry.

My muscles complained that I had not done enough riding recently, but despite that I managed to haul myself into the saddle.

My horse bunched his muscles when he felt my weight and

made to drop his head between his knees, but I was determined that he would not. I hauled his head up and he swung it from side to side, but the worst he could manage was a single crow-hop before things commenced to happen.

I did not see a signal, nor did I hear a command. But suddenly, muskets boomed and rifles cracked, the flashes visible in the dimness despite the powder-smoke that soon clouded the scene. Our untrained horses bucked, frightened by the noise and the smell, but we soon got them under control and fired back.

I had no proper target to aim at in the dimness, so I pointed my rifle to where I'd spotted movement and squeezed hard on that stiff front trigger. The rifle jolted me, for in the excitement of controlling both my horse and my rifle, I had not thought to pull the butt tightly against my shoulder.

I never got the chance to reload.

A shot came from out of the darkness and struck my horse. I heard the thump and felt him stagger, so I knew he had been hit hard. I kicked my feet free of the stirrups, intending to jump clear, but there was no time.

He tried to whinny, I think, but it turned into a loud grunt as he fell, not quite dead but clearly dying. I was unable to roll clear or pull myself from under him, for he had landed on my right leg, trapping it.

His dying lunges caused me so much pain that I lost my senses and never felt Jean-Louis and two men lift his dead weight, just enough for another to pull my leg free. But when he did, I woke me from my swoon and almost screamed from the pain.

Jean-Louis held me by the shoulders while Juan Vargas, who had gained his knowledge from caring for horses, moved my knee around to see whether it was broken.

Someone handed me a half-full flask of whiskey and I drank two hefty swallows, which soon reduced my agony to a throbbing pain. I was then able to lift my head and look at the swollen knee for a moment before leaning back against Jean-Louis, cold sweat beading my brow.

"Ain't broke, I figure," Juan said. "If he don't go jumping

creeks or some other fool stunt, I reckon he'll soon be as good as new."

I was so relieved that I shared what was left of the whiskey with him.

When he handed it back, now empty, I saw the owner's initials on it, JHM. I handed it to John Moore and promised to refill it with whiskey as soon as I was able, or good French brandy if that was his choice.

He just grinned at me and promised that we'd talk after I recovered.

***

A parley had gone on while I was unconscious, back and forth between Lieutenant Castañeda and John Moore. Castañeda wanted to know why we'd attacked without warning. John then invited him to join us and defend the Constitution of 1824. Castañeda declined, then offered to leave if John gave up our old cannon, which was the first we knew of why they'd come.

I wondered later on if John had actually said to him, "Come and take it!"

The parley broke up after that and fighting resumed for a time, as I found out later, but by then I was on my way back to Gonzales and grateful to Doc Whiskey for sparing me much pain. Honesty bids me confess that I had *two* pains the following morning, only one of which had been caused by my horse falling on me.

Lieutenant Castañeda soon realized that he lacked the men and guns to do as he'd been ordered, so he broke off the attack and headed back to Bexar to present his excuses.

Our men then did their best to drink up all the whiskey in Gonzales.

They were welcome to it as far as I was concerned, for I can attest that whatever that foul stuff was, it truly dishonored the name of whiskey!

Jack L Knapp

Chapter Nine

Men from places like San Felipe off to the east had wanted to get into the fight, but got to Gonzales too late, and more than one wanted me to replace a loose lock-spring or just tighten things up in general. Unlike the local folks, they had cash money, so I was glad for the business.

I also got caught up on what was going on back east. Santa Anna had taken charge down in Mexico City and the Constitution of 1824 had been set aside. He hadn't made himself king yet, as some thought he might, but things that had been left up to the states were now being decided by his Centralists, so in practical terms I figured it didn't matter what he called himself.

What *did* matter was whether the new government would recognize land titles, such as they were. I heard from one of the new arrivals that a ring of thieves back east had got their hands on a bunch of signed grants. A speculator could pay them a few dollars if he had 'em, maybe even swap an old horse for the paper if he didn't.

The ring's agent would then fill in the details and hand the speculator a paper granting him title to ten leagues of good land! Which he could then sell to anybody, Mexican citizen or not, seeing as how the whole thing was crooked to start with.

When the new owner showed up to register his title, he found out that he'd been swindled. By then, the scoundrel who had taken his money was long gone.

No question, the signature of the Mexican official was genuine, so most hired a lawyer to see what could be done.

As it turned out, not much, for despite that signature the Centralists had finally figured out that all those new American settlers didn't care a fig for Mexico or what Santa Anna wanted.

So there would be trouble, maybe even a war with the United

States if they decided to support the settlers. There had already been disagreements over the boundaries of the Louisiana Purchase and neither side was satisfied with how things had turned out.

The solution, as the Centralists saw it, was to take away the settlers' guns before they used them on Mexicans.

Including that nearly-useless old cannon.

I was up and around but still limping when Steven F. Austin showed up on October 11th to take command.

That's when I knowed that the fight that had cost me a horse and paid me with a gimpy knee wasn't over. Austin was an important man, not one to be getting involved over nothing much.

The skirmish had showed folks that the Mexican government was serious about disarming us. The politicians down in Mexico City either had no experience fighting Indians or didn't care, but either way they'd left us no choice.

We would have to fight, and Austin wasn't the sort of hombre to let the grass grow under his feet. He was already gathering men to run Mexico out of Texas for good.

I liked the sound of that. We'd built homes and businesses and towns, now we would build our own nation! Despite my sore knee, I intended to be part of it.

I made up my mind that when Austin led our men west, I would go along even if I had to ride in a wagon.

Edward Burleson was back in town, now a lieutenant-colonel in command of Austin-township's militia. But when I offered to join up, he turned me down.

"Jake, we'll be marching from here to San Antonio de Bexar. There's no way you can keep up with your knee the way it is, and I can't afford to lose what men I've got taking care of you when your leg gives out. But that doesn't mean you can't help the cause. My boys are fighters, but some only have shotguns or old muskets and that won't be nearly good enough to drive the Mexicans out of Bexar. They are short of money, but I'd take it kindly if you'd fix what is needed anyway."

I agreed that I would, and the next day when customers started arriving, it turned out that not a one of them could pay!

***

Ed brought Steven Austin around, and while we were looking at some of the guns the militia intended to fight with, several of the town's ladies showed up with food. A man I didn't know spread a cowhide in front of my cabin and we sat down and ate. While we did, we talked over what Austin and Sam Houston had in mind.

"Santa Anna has two choices, the way we see it," Steven said. "He can cross at Laredo and bring his army up to Bexar, which they hold, and from there turn east.

"He'll stick to the old Camino Real, then," I said, "but he might cross at Matamoros instead of Laredo. From there, he'd follow the Atascocito Road north of Nueces Bay and turn east through Victoria and Goliad. You might want to send a few scouts down there to make sure Santa Anna doesn't sneak past you."

They exchanged a glance, then the conversation turned to other things. I figured they weren't impressed by my opinion, but they seemed to be interested in me or at least in my gunsmithing.

A few minutes later, Ed looked at Steven, who nodded back like they'd reached some sort of agreement without my knowing.

"Jake, you can't march, but can you sit a saddle?" Steven asked.

"I reckon," I said. "I've done a lot of standing at my bench lately and the knee is holding up all right. It's a mite sore late in the day and early in the morning, but it's getting better. You're thinking I could join up with George Kimbell's ranging company?"

"No, something else," Steven said. "How well do you know the country around Galveston? What about north of there?" Ed asked.

"Better than most, I'd say. I crossed from Louisiana quite a few times, most often from Alexandria to San Augustine, but we made a couple of trips to Nacogdoches too. Why do you ask?"

"I've got a people's army that's short of everything, including people," Ed explained. "I intend to take Bexar, but I don't have enough men to stop Santa Anna if he gets past me. Indians are a problem, too; raids started to pick up as soon as they realized that there was no one to stop them.

"I'm thinking of our women and children. With the men off fighting, they're worried because they'll be left without protection and a man that's concerned for his family won't be able to concentrate on fighting Santa Anna. I've already been approached by several, wondering what I propose to do about it."

"I can understand that," I said, "but what does that have to do with me?"

"If we don't manage to stop Santa Anna out here, there's not a single strong point closer than the eastern settlements. We'll be forced to retreat, probably all the way to the Sabine, and we won't have time to round up our families and take them with us. Leaving them to the mercy of Mexican soldiers...well, it doesn't bear thinking about.

"The ones that have talked to me, I want you to guide their families east and see that they're safe during the trip. Will you do that?"

"I don't know, Ed. One man...I could talk to Jean-Louis, I'm sure he'd go with me, but even so..."

"Jake, if you were taking care of their families, I'll bet that I could get another two or three hundred men to volunteer! I know you'd rather be part of the fighting, but you're still not fit and even if you were, you'd only be one more rifleman. It makes sense for you to take the families that are ready now east. It would be one less thing I'd have to worry about."

Persuasive hombres, Ed Burleson and Steven Austin! They talked me into it.

I figured they had it easier, what with only having to organize an army and fight the Mexicans.

Women? And children, maybe a few old codgers that didn't want to wait around to starve because there was no one to do for them? As soon as I gave them my word, I started regretting that I had. But I reckoned I could do it. Ten or a dozen women, maybe less...

People out on the frontier, especially those farther out than we were, were pretty self-reliant. I figured Ed might be unduly alarmed, but a man doesn't go back on his pledged word.

No matter how much he might want to.

My first job was to talk Jean-Louis out of joining the Gonzales Ranging Company and instead, help me chivvy a dozen women and kids all the way to east Texas.

"I'd rather herd sheep!" was one of his milder objections, but I wore him down. Took me a while and the best part of a bottle of French brandy, but the next morning he showed up at daylight, ready to get started.

He brought with him two men who'd been breaking horses for him on the ranch and about thirty horses, most the mounts he'd loaned out during that scrap with Lieutenant Castañeda's men. The rest were ones that he figured were broke well enough to pull a wagon.

The four of us would require spare mounts on the trip and there was no telling what sort of animals the families would have. Chances were that if they had any, their best animals had gone with their men when they joined up.

Ed's militia were infantry, not because they liked to take long walks, but because none of them owned horses. Most people who lived in town didn't; they just rented one from the livery stable when it was needed.

I'd thought of doing that myself, but I had the corral out back and people needing horseshoeing or gun-work were happy to pay me with a load of hay or a bushel of corn. So I'd asked Jean-Louis and he'd brought me a horse, which I almost never got the chance to ride.

We turned the horses they'd brought into the corral, except for two, and Jean-Louis headed off with them to Austin town. I figured the trip might take him two days, maybe only one if he swapped a tired horse for a fresh one along the way. He would let folks know that we proposed to guide folks east to safety, then turn southwest and loop around letting others know on his way back to Gonzales.

Ed had given some of his men leave to go bring their families in, so they showed up at my shop wanting to borrow horses.

I was busy working in the shop at the time and never saw

them; Jean-Louis's men saw to loaning them mounts. I went out to the corral that evening to see to feeding and watering a herd of twenty or more and was some perplexed to find only half a dozen draft animals!

I had figured to work on the guns until the families showed up. After we saw how many we were dealing with, we could decide what to do next. Eight or ten women and their kids? I reckoned that the four of us could handle that many.

I arranged to borrow Clem Satterlee's wagon the next morning and made the rounds of Gonzales that afternoon, looking for any food that people could spare. It fair gave me a lump in my throat the way they responded when I told them why I wanted it. They brought out hams, bacon sides, jerky, cornmeal for us and shelled corn for the animals, preserved fruits, and honey.

And of course, Jean-Louis and me would hunt during the trip after we set up camp. The other two men would keep watch to make sure no Indian or road-agent showed up to cause trouble.

A week later, we had the makings of a new town camped out east of Gonzales. It was hard to keep track of all those kids running around, but we figured close to *sixty* women!

The good thing was that some had wagons and others had regular carriages! The bad thing was that they expected to haul everything they owned, except for their houses, with them.

I put a stop to that in a hurry, but you'd have thought I was telling them to leave their kids behind!

Finally, I called a meeting and laid down the law. "We've got a long, hard trip ahead of us. Those of you with carriages, expect to share with a passenger or two, more'n likely one or two women with babies. Smaller children will ride in the wagons, older ones will ride horses or walk. Some already have horses and for the ones that don't but know how to ride, I'll do my best to round up a horse for them.

"I prefer that you work things out between yourselves if you can, but if you can't I'll do it for you. You need to understand one thing up front. I'm in charge on this trip, and Jean-Louis speaks for me. If you don't like it, then you're welcome to head out on your own. But out there on the road, there'll be dangers and no one to help if you get in trouble."

Well, they didn't like that, especially the ones related to the Old Three Hundred settlers that had come in with Steven Austin. I was informed that I was a nobody with not even a labor of land of my own, and who did I think I was to be ordering them around? They kept on complaining, especially when I ordered Abe and Jessie, the two men Jean-Louis had brought from his spread, to unload their wagons.

Most houses in Gonzales had extra room inside for some of the more valuable items, and every house had covered porches out front. Pretty soon, those porches sported chairs and boxes of stuff. Mine did too, so that when I sat down to rest at the end of the day I no longer had to sit on the ground and lean back against the log wall.

Other chairs didn't stay empty either. Most of the ones going with me were town folk, not accustomed to sitting on the ground. Libby Sanders, the wife of one of Ed's militiamen, showed up with her daughter Priscilla to sit that first night, and what could I do? I offered to let them stay in my cabin until we left and I unrolled my blankets on the floor of my shop.

Will Sanders and one of his friends stopped by with a bottle that evening and they had a good cackle at my predicament.

Nice fellows, they were, and we emptied that bottle before they left. While we were talking, Will told me that he and a partner owned a hat store in Austin. He promised me a real hat when I got back.

But I never got it.

He was killed a few weeks later during the fighting around Bexar.

Chapter Ten

I wanted to get an early start, but it seemed like there were way too many things that hadn't gotten done yet.

Or so the women insisted. It was irritating, but Jean-Louis calmed me down some and between the four of us urging them on, we finally rolled out of Gonzales.

Will's daughter Priscilla rode with me that first morning, out in front of the gaggle of wagons and sort-of riders that hadn't figured out their proper place in the column yet. Jean-Louis had picked out a gelding for her that was a little older and calmer than most, and since she was riding out where we might run into difficulties I gave her one of my pistols and showed her how to load and fire it.

I also pointed out that she would have one shot at the most, being inexperienced and slow at reloading, so she should plan on spurring that gelding back to the wagons while I stayed back and slowed down whoever figured to cause trouble.

The day passed quietly, except for the foofaraw a time or two when some woman that figured she was important objected to eating the dust of her inferior up ahead. Jean-Louis quieted them down better than I could, seeing as how he had a way with words that I couldn't match. Comes from being fluent in at least three languages, I expect. I could make myself understood in French and was better with Spanish, but there were times when American speech failed me.

His manners were fit to charm a king, too, while mine were apt to enrage a mule. Not that they needed much encouragement, being born ornery and growing up to be worse.

Priscilla was pleasant company and right pretty I thought, but she was younger than most I'd talked with on my way west. Hardly more than a child I figured, although no child filled out that homespun shirt the way she did. Which left me nearly speechless the first time I noticed.

I pushed on, following what Steven Austin had named the Camino Arriba, and not allowing a stop until mid-afternoon. By then, the old biddies most apt to cause a ruckus were tired enough and cold enough to have settled down.

I led the way off to the side of the road and between us four men, we got the wagons into a square. We unhitched, then brought all of our stock inside except for two fresh horses for Jean-Louis and me, which we tied to a wagon tongue while we got ready to hunt.

Abe and Jesse rustled dry oak wood for the fire and convinced the women to organize themselves for cooking and cleaning up afterwards, while Jean-Louis and me rode out ahead about half a mile. We dismounted and headed up a creek to find game.

We had been taking turns, one hunting, the other leading the horses. That was why I was the one that surprised a buffalo cow and a yearling drinking at the creek. I shot the cow, figuring that I'd only get one chance and the yearling might not have meat enough for everyone.

The sound of that gunshot spooked a herd of around twenty others that I hadn't seen, and they took off immediately, with the yearling doing his best to catch up.

It took us two trips to get everything back to the wagons, the first time hauling nothing but meat, the second with one horse packing meat and the other the hide. Heavy, it was, and that horse was plumb tuckered out by the time we got to the wagons.

A buffalo robe, if I could find someone to tan it for me, was warm enough even for a Texas norther. If I couldn't get it tanned, I figured to scrape all the meat off that hide and after it dried, use it for a rug.

We had been too busy to talk much on that second trip, but after we got back Jean-Louis complained that I was having all the luck on this trip.

I pointed out that it could just as easily have been him that spotted that buffalo, but it turned out that wasn't what was bothering him. "Jake, you're out front riding with Priscilla while

I'm stuck back there with a bunch of old women that would scare a Comanche to death! I'd like for us to switch places tomorrow."

I hadn't thought about it, but I guessed it made sense. After all, we'd both come down this branch of the road on our way to Gonzales, so he knew the way as well as I did.

Next morning, he rode off with Priscilla as soon as we'd eaten. They were soon out of sight, because we couldn't leave that campground until Abe and Jesse had finished greasing a wheel hub.

Which left me with nothing to do but stand around looking dumb and listening to the women complain about this, that, and the other.

A time or two I spotted Abe and Jesse grinning at me, and when I scowled at them they just grinned wider. A body would think they'd already forgot which one of us had hard money to pay them their wages!

We continued to swap jobs for the next few days, Jean-Louis and me. Late afternoons, after we'd made camp and were waiting to eat, I noticed that some of the time Priscilla sat by Jean-Louis after she'd collected her meal. Other times, she sat with me, her mother keeping a close eye on us all the time.

There was a lot more talking going on when she was with Jean-Louis than when she was with me. Seemed like she smiled more often too, which bothered me some though I couldn't figure out why.

When she started to join me out in front a week later, I told her that today it was better if she stayed back with the wagons. I gave as my excuse that we were getting close to where Indians might show up, but the truth is I was feeling grumpy and just felt like riding alone.

It didn't help, because it turned out that I was bothered that day by having no one to talk to. And I wasn't surprised when she huddled close to the fire that evening with Jean-Louis. Talking a mile a minute, she was, and laughing up a storm.

But then Jesse called me over to look at an axle on one of the wagons. It had developed a lengthwise split, and after that I got too involved in discussing whether a rawhide wrap might hold it together long enough to reach the next town to think about her.

Jesse rode alongside of the wagons with me next day, one or the other of us staying back to keep an eye on that axle. I figured we could make a replacement if we had to, seeing as there was plenty of post-oaks growing in clumps along the road, but it would cost us time we couldn't spare.

For sickness had showed up, and I was worried.

I called a council that afternoon after we set up camp.

"Four people are already down with the chills and fever, and the weather is likely to get worse before it gets better. Abe, I need you and Jesse to take over as drivers, including one on that wagon with the worrisome axle. The other will drive a wagon with the sickest ones so they can rest.

"Jean-Louis and I will stay mounted and keep an eye on things, but don't worry if you don't see us right away. We won't be far away if anything happens.

"I figure to take the most direct way to San Felipe we can find and see about replacing that axle there. If they've got a doctor to care for our sick, we may leave them until they get better. Meanwhile, we need to do a better job of keeping our folks warm and dry. Once we get to Liberty, I'll see how many the residents can take in. After that, I'll decide whether to cross the Sabine or go north to Nacogdoches and as soon as everyone is safe, I'll head back to San Felipe for the ones we left behind. I don't like the idea, because it will mean spending more time out on the road, but I didn't set a time limit on how long I'd be gone when I agreed to see the families to safety.

"Our animals are still in reasonable shape, but we'll need to keep a close eye on them. Judging by the clouds, I wouldn't be surprised to see rain or maybe snow tomorrow; I don't reckon it matters which, because either one will slow us down."

"Jake, we might have to stop for a while, maybe even build shelters," Jean-Louis interrupted. "If it snows, the horses won't be able to find enough grass."

"Won't take us long to put up a lean-to if that happens," I agreed, "and there's plenty of good firewood nearby. Oak burns hot and the coals last a long time."

***

The next morning, we woke to a cold drizzle. It was a miserable start to the day and it got worse later, even after the sun came out. Mud gripped the wheels and finally that weakened axle gave out.

We set up camp where it happened and started rearranging. Food and warm clothing was a priority, caring for the animals another. I apportioned out some of the corn and worried that the rest might not last us until we got to San Felipe.

The next morning, I got called by Abe to old Missus Wheeler's wagon.

She had been one of the sick ones, and finally cold and exhaustion had got to be too much for her. We buried her body alongside the road, not the first time that that had happened, although she was the first we'd lost.

We put up a simple cross of oak branches tied together with rawhide strips, I said a few words over the mound, and then we loaded everyone in the wagons and pulled away.

I looked back at that lonely cross more'n once. I 'spect others did too, but then we passed a stand of trees and I couldn't see it any more.

***

Two days later, we lost Joseph Fletcher and Addie Ross. Addie had been sick, so her passing was no surprise, but Joe had looked to be in better shape than most. He had just stepped down from his wagon that evening, when suddenly he grabbed at his chest and fell down. By the time we got to him, he was dead.

Her children wouldn't hear of the two of them sharing a grave, so we buried them side by side the next morning though it meant more digging for us. We set up two more crosses, I spoke a few words over the mounds, and we pushed on.

***

The people of San Felipe made a fuss over the women and children, which pleased all of us. The last two that had been sick decided they were well enough to keep going, but I figured they would do better with a couple of days rest. The horses also needed time to recover.

While we waited, we caught up on the news. There had been more fighting, some of it over by Bexar, but also down near Goliad. We felt guilty at not being there, but four more riflemen wouldn't have made a difference.

We knowed that, but shirking his duty makes a man want to wash harder to wipe out the stain. Not that he ever can.

I fidgeted, Jean-Louis talked to Priscilla, and the horses regained some of the flesh they'd lost, thanks to the good hay and corn we fed them.

I tried to thank the people who'd donated it, but they shrugged it off. I reckon they knew that the rest and good feed might be the difference in whether we made it to Liberty or not.

We made it to Liberty without losing any more people, but that was the only good thing about the last part of that miserable trip. A busted single-tree that we replaced, leather harness rotted by the wet with not enough time to dry, or for that matter, tallow to keep the leather supple…

By the end of it, Jean-Louis and me were snapping at each other so bad that only Abe and Jesse holding us back prevented a fight.

Next morning, neither one of us wanted to talk to the other, but being older Abe and Jesse gave us both what-for and we apologized just in time to wish Priscilla a happy fifteenth birthday.

But as soon as we'd unhitched in Liberty, Abe and Jesse let us know they had had enough of our fussing.

They hadn't decided whether to go north to Nacogdoches or south to Galveston, but we gave them a horse each and our thanks, with a promise that we'd find work for them if we should ever run into them again.

The rest of our horses we sold, except four that we'd need to make it back to Gonzales.

Weakened as they were, we figured to swap off as often as necessary and rest them when they couldn't go on.

We shared out the money we got from selling the others with the folks we'd brought east. Little enough it was, but it was the best we could do and they were glad to get it.

The sun was just beginning to show the next morning when we started for home.

***

We stopped to ask for a meal when we had the chance, lived on what we shot the rest of the time. Took us a week before we started talking to each other more than was absolutely needful.

But I was feeling ashamed and I reckon Jean-Louis was too, so gradually things got better.

The news we got during our stops wasn't good.

Steven Austin had wanted to attack Bexar directly, but Sam Houston and some others wanted to wait long enough to teach the new men what they needed to know. He also pointed out that they needed more cannon. While they argued back and forth, more men arrived.

Old Ben Milam and a few others had paid more attention than the leaders and decided to start without them.

There had been heavy fighting after that and we realized that we had likely lost friends. Knowing John Moore and Ed Burleson the way we did, we knew that both would have been in the thick of things. Jim Bowie, too, if he hadn't managed to get himself killed in a previous scrape.

Some thought he wanted to die and hadn't figured out a way just yet without blowing his own head off. Which, as a Catholic he wouldn't do, because the church wouldn't allow him to be buried with the family he missed so much.

I didn't have a death wish, neither did Jean-Louis, but we pushed on hard because we felt like we should do our part of the fighting. We figured to stop in Gonzales just long enough to pick up fresh horses before going on to Bexar, but it turned out that we weren't needed. I felt guilty about not being there and relieved, then felt guilty again because I felt relieved.

I wondered whether Jean-Louis felt the same way, then decided he didn't. It just wasn't in me to be as brave as some.

Burnet, the interim president, had sent Steven Austin off to

Washington to see if the Americans would help. That left Ed Burleson as the new army commander in Bexar, and his Texian forces, along with Juan Seguin and a company of Tejanos, had forced the surrender of General Cos. It had happened less than a week before we rode into Gonzales.

With the fighting over, some of the volunteers had headed back for home, sure that the war was won. Others had stayed in Bexar to keep Cos from coming back.

So we got back to what we'd been doing before.

Jean-Louis recruited a few new hands to help him round up and break horses. They set off for his place the next morning and I set to work in my shop. A local man had taken care of the blacksmithing while we'd been gone, using my tools and equipment, which I didn't care for because he'd moved hammers and tongs and such around to where I couldn't lay my hands on them right away. He'd also used up most of my stock of charcoal, which really got my dander up, until he paid me half of what he'd taken in.

Gradually, everything returned to normal in Gonzales Town.

That was when Santa Anna crossed the border with his army.

Chapter Eleven

We'd got back to Gonzales in time for Christmas, but nobody felt like celebrating. We knowed that Santa Anna was in Texas, but had no idea where he intended to go.

From time to time, I wondered how the folks I left back in the east were doing. Priscilla's mother hadn't fared well during the trip and her husband had been killed at Bexar, but had she found out yet? And what of Priscilla?

I'd thought at one point that I might court her after the trip was over, but she'd seemed more interested in Jean-Louis. Not surprising, because he was better looking and could talk a turkey off its roost. But it left me with an ache that only work helped me put aside.

So it was a good thing that I had more work than I'd ever had, enough to keep me and the two assistants I'd hired going from daybreak to dark.

Jean-Louis was busy too; he'd hired several men as soon as we got back. One was a cook, another was charged with bringing in firewood for what looked to be a hard winter, and the rest were busy rounding up and breaking mustangs.

We were as short of cash money to pay them as anyone, but there were plenty of young men looking for work. He promised to feed them and provide each one with a mount after the breaking was done.

That might not have seemed like much a year ago, but a year ago Santa Anna's lancers were on the far side of the Rio Grande. Now? Having a horse might keep a man alive if the Mexicans came through Gonzales.

But both of us were out here and Priscilla was back there.

A pretty young girl like her? She would likely have found herself a beau among the young men of Nacogdoches or Liberty by now. She might even be married! I tried not to think about it, and some of the time I didn't.

***

Folks had been certain that we'd get all the help we needed from the United States, but so far all we'd seen was a handful of volunteers.

There was a consultation going on back at San Felipe, but since the politicians lacked the nerve to declare independence, most figured they were shirkers happy to leave the fighting to better men.

Ed Burleson was still in charge of the volunteers, and he was doing his best to hold things together, but a lot of Texas men had headed for home as soon as the fight was over. Some had stayed in San Antonio de Bexar to keep the Mexicans from re-occupying the place, but like the ones who'd already gone, most had farms and families to take care of. How long they would remain was anybody's guess.

Folks had begun to mention Sam Houston recently.

He had been off in the east, negotiating a peace treaty with the Cherokees, but he showed up at Washington-on-the-Brazos in time for the Assembly to finally declare that Texas was independent from Mexico, if we could make it stick. The other thing the Assembly had done was appoint Houston, who at one time had been a major general in command of Tennessee's militia, to be major general of the Texian army.

So far, the army didn't exist, but the ones I talked to figured that if anybody could raise one, Sam could.

For one thing, he was a close friend of President Andy Jackson, but since Jackson was about to leave office it would be up to Martin Van Buren to decide whether he wanted to send American soldiers to help us. He didn't have many to start with and most were busy fighting Indians. The Seminoles in Florida were particularly troublesome.

I soon found out that Houston hadn't waited for Van Buren to make up his mind.

He showed up in Gonzales with the men he'd talked into joining up and was doing his best to turn them from a mob into soldiers. Now and then, he sent some to have me fix their rifles.

But on March the thirteenth, he ran out of time. That was when Susanna Dickinson brought word that the Alamo had fallen.

Most of the defenders had died fighting, and the ones who hadn't had been immediately executed. We had been worried up to the time we heard about it. Now, we were mad clear through and I was as determined as any to make them pay.

That evening, after the work in the smithy and the gun-shop was done, I started in to mold bullets. Those one-pound pigs of lead wouldn't do me a bit of good, but the bullets I made from them might.

Some others realized what I was doing and asked to join in, so I shared my lead with them. Having a man with bullets fighting on your side sure beat having one with no bullets.

One of them brought me a nice Indian-tanned buffalo robe. Turned out that I never made a better swap in my life.

Ed Burleson brought Houston around to the shop and I laid down the rifle I was converting and shook hands.

Big, he was, but maybe that was what was needed, a big man who could get things done.

Houston didn't waste any time. "Ed told me about you taking that train of women and children back to Nacogdoches."

"I wish I could have done better," I said. "We lost people on that trip and some got sick."

"I heard about your sick people in San Felipe, and I don't know of anyone who could have done a better job! Matter of fact, the way I see it, anybody that could manage a job like that ought to be a captain. Ed? He's rightly one of yours."

"I agree, Sam. Jake, you're now a captain of volunteers, not because of what you did, but because we need a captain. The thing is, we want you to do it again."

I balled up my fists for a moment. I swear, if there hadn't of been two of them and Houston so big, I would have punched Ed in the face!

But I kept my anger inside, mostly. "I plan on being here and helping defend my town if the Mexicans come this way," I said coldly. "Herding women and old men is a thankless job at best and

I got a bellyful when I did it before. Get someone else to do it now!"

"Nope. Couple of reasons," said Houston calmly, "starting with the fact that you won't have a town to defend. Tomorrow morning, I'm sending everyone that can't fight east, and unless I have someone who knows what he's doing to lead that train, a lot of them will die."

"What do you mean, I won't have a town to defend?" I didn't like the sound of that; I'd put a lot of sweat and a fair amount of blood into building my house and my business.

"The army can't stop them, Jake. That's the plain truth; there are too many of them, too few of us, and our men figure that an order is a suggestion. Which, most of the time, they don't figure to obey.

"So before Santa Anna gets here and starts handing your property over to his officers, I've made up my mind to burn Gonzales to the ground. Just as soon as you head east, my men will start lighting the fires. And after everything is burning good, every house, every shop, and every outhouse, the army will follow you. The only ones behind us will be a ranging company to act as scouts."

For a moment, I didn't think he was serious.

But Ed had a grim look about him when he nodded and I understood that Houston meant just what he'd said.

"We're sending *everybody* out, Jake. The women and kids will go on ahead, and if you don't drive them hard we'll pass you up. What few men we've got…well, we can't afford to lose any. If we end up getting pushed across the Sabine, families will need their menfolk."

I was shocked, but I wanted to make them understand what they were telling me to do.

"Ed, I can't do this! We were four, and there were times I thought we weren't going to make it! Winter ain't over yet, it's been raining, and if a norther blows in we'll be bucking snowdrifts.

"I can lead the willing ones east, but I wouldn't bet a plugged nickel that any of us will get as far as San Felipe. Just for starters, how am I supposed to feed them? What happens when they get sick?

"I'm no doctor, the only way some got better on that last trip is because Abe found a bay tree and later on a sassafras. He knew how to make the tea, which none of us had ever heard of. That tea, and the honey we used to sweeten it, saved lives. How many are you talking about, anyway? Fifty, maybe sixty?"

"Jake, you've been so busy in your shop that I reckon you haven't noticed," Houston said. "We've got at least a hundred here in Gonzales right now, and more coming every day."

I could tell that I wasn't going to convince Houston, but Ed Burleson knew me. He knew I wasn't one to shy away from a shadow, so I talked to him.

"Ed, I can't do it. I just *can't*. I would if I could, but it's too much for any man." I turned to Houston. "Sam, you don't know what you're asking."

"You'll have help, Jake. Pick two lieutenants and have them round up some assistants, say half a dozen apiece. You'll also need a hunting party out ahead, and scouts to make sure the Indians don't cause problems. We'll give you as much help as we can."

I could tell that I wasn't going to talk them out of this, and in the end, I reckoned that I wouldn't want to face their problems. Mine looked to be bad enough!

***

My helpers and me went through Gonzales, gathering everything we thought we'd need and telling the women to show up at the east side of town as early as possible if they planned to go with us.

Wagons, carts, buggies, anything that didn't have a soldier guarding it, I collected up. Along the way, I sent a man out to tell Jean-Louis to bring in everything he could carry and drive in every horse they had, broke or not. And when he left, to set fire to his place.

I made up my mind to do the same thing in the morning. If my home and shop was to be burned, I was going to do it myself.

I could have used a week, deciding what went and who was to do which job. I got about four hours before it was too dark to do much, and finally I laid down on my buffalo robe and tried to sleep. Maybe I did.

But I was tired and short-tempered when I woke up. One of the men I'd selected to ride ahead as part of a wood detail objected, and I hit him in the face harder than I ought to have and knocked him down, but after that people got quiet and did what they were told.

Jean-Louis and his hunters were already on the road ahead of us when we rolled out. He'd offered to take over the wood-gathering too, which I was glad of because it meant that all I had to do was get everyone else moving.

Telling them that there would be a campsite ready when we got to it, with wood and fresh meat waiting to be cooked for our supper, helped. So did the news of what Santa Anna's men had done at the Alamo.

We were a grim lot that left Gonzales that morning, determined that if the Mexicans caught up to us they wouldn't take anyone alive. Men talked openly to friends, asking them to do what they might not be able to do themselves if wounded or too sick to fight: hand them a loaded gun, and if they were in no condition to pull the trigger themselves, to do it for them.

I didn't ask that of Jean-Louis, nor did he mention it to me. We'd been together long enough that it went without saying.

***

An hour after we left, the fog rolled in and after that, it started raining. A cold drizzle that might turn into snow it was, and until it did the cold ate deep into our bones.

We hunched our shoulders and pulled our caps down tight. The ones that had shawls wrapped them around their necks to stay as warm as possible, and I wished I had one.

A mile further down the road, I rode up behind a woman driving a wagon. She was trying to shelter her two youngsters, four or five years old I figured, and she was holding them in front to protect them with her own body.

So I headed back to the wagon with my stuff and picked up the buffalo robe I'd counted on to keep me warm on the trip. I untied the strings as I rode forward, and by the time I reached her, I had it unrolled. I leaned out of my saddle and draped it across her shoulders and when I did, she started crying.

The time to cry was when she was cold and wet and her kids were shivering, I figured! But no, she'd waited until I laid that buffalo robe over her!

I reckon there's no understanding women.

Chapter Twelve

The fog returned during the night, which made us colder and more miserable.

I shivered, felt sorry for myself for giving up my buffalo robe, and made up my mind to speak to Jean-Louis and his hunters. If there was any chance at all to kill a few buffalo, I wanted them to take it. Bears would be equally welcome, because they also had thick, warm pelts.

There would be no time to tan them until after we got to Nacogdoches, but even a dried skin makes a warm pallet. And it would free up whatever quilts or blankets the families owned so that they could use them for coverings.

But the fog hung on until nearly noon and after it lifted, clouds blocked the sun. No buffalo, and no bears.

It was cold all afternoon, and then the fog came back. The hunters drifted in to camp late and empty-handed. Finally, just before dark, a distant boom announced that someone had at least shot *at* something.

I made the rounds from wagon to wagon and noticed that while they waited, the families that had food were sharing what they had with their neighbors. Not much, and not nearly enough, I figured, but they were doing what they could.

Hungry children cried and their mothers tried to soothe them, not that it helped. I kept on moving, trying to get back to the last third of the wagons where there were only old people so I wouldn't have to listen to the little ones.

It didn't help. The oldsters just looked at me, eyes empty. I reckon they'd been hungry before, as hungry as me.

A man can't put his hungry out of mind.

It's always there, until just before starvation sets in. By then, you've lost whatever fat you had and your stomach has shrunk down to the size of an apple. You're a short step away from dying, but at least you're not hungry anymore.

Or so claimed the old mountain men, who'd been that bad off a time or two.

I wasn't there yet, so my empty belly kept on gnawing at me. I looked up in the bare trees to see if hungry squirrels and possums had missed anything, a persimmon or maybe a hickory nut, but if they had I didn't see it. And I looked long and hard, just in case.

Finally, the last two hunters walked into camp. Their horses were packing the butchered carcass of a small pony and they were none too pleased to be doing it.

In better times, most of our people would have turned up their nose at horsemeat, and several of the men refused to cook their portions. Women, being more practical, put their pride aside and broiled their portions. The children ate it without knowing or caring what kind of meat it was, and soon most women joined them, the nursing mothers going first.

I ate mine, not that our portions were more than a mouthful, and so did Jean-Louis. We'd eaten worse a time or two after Uncle Henry ran out of fresh meat and vegetables for the *Eureka*'s crew. What was in those casks might actually have *been* salt horse, as some of the crew claimed. I'd figured they were just having fun with the greenhorn at the time, but I'd never been sure.

It was the first time during the trip that we had nothing to eat but horsemeat, but it wasn't the last. The next time, the ones that had refused it joined in with the rest of us.

Next morning, the sun was out by the time we were ready to leave.

I sent the hunters on ahead and told them to find the first camping place where they could hunt.

They did, and jumped a herd of elk, killing seven before they got out of range. We got there in mid-afternoon and by then, only two carcasses were still hanging; the rest had been butchered and the meat was waiting, sliced and ready for cooking.

The hunters had already had some, and some had had more than they ought to on an empty stomach. But there was plenty for the rest of us and the greedy ones paid for it. Now and then, you'd see one holding onto his belly as he hobbled behind the nearest tree.

I saw to it that the elk-hides went to the ones that needed them most. Not enough for me to have one, but maybe next time, or the time after that...

Two days later, we were once again short of food.

The mesquite brush alongside the trail attracted deer, which browsed on the fresh green tips of branches, but the pair that the men bagged didn't go very far.

Most mothers went without so that their children could have as much as possible, but even so it wasn't enough.

The next day turned out to be more of the same.

I was as worried as anyone, because hunger was not my only concern. People had come down with the chills and fever. Some were old folks, but children made up more than half of the sick ones. The only thing we could do was push on ahead and hope things got better.

They didn't.

The next morning, we waited around just long enough to bury the middle-aged woman and little girl who had died sometime during the night. Our mood was grim when we drove on, for the animals were also showing the strain. Just looking at the saddle stock, where every rib was showing, was enough to make men turn away and wipe their eyes.

Later that afternoon, three men headed for me. They had never shirked, doing all a man could expect of them to keep the wagons moving, but I could see that they had reached their breaking point.

August Smith was the first to speak, and his right hand hung down near his pistol while he did.

"Goddamn it, we can't keep on doing this! Jake, we've got to stop and let the animals rest or they'll start dying on us! Two or three days is all I'm asking; it will give us time to spread farther out and find some game. My family will die if we don't!"

"Gus, you've got how many?" I asked. "Your wife, her grandmother, and three kids?"

Gus nodded, still angry but willing to talk. "The kids got at least a little bit to eat last night. Jake, I ain't had a decent meal in over a week and my wife has gone without about that long."

Neither had I, and for a moment I felt like hitting him. For that matter, all three of them, and if it came to a shooting scrape...

But I forced my anger down before it got out of control.

Maybe, if I had been in his place, I'd feel the same way.

"Gus, I'm hungry too," I said. "We all are. You're trying to take care of five people, but I'm responsible for more than a hundred. You want to trade jobs?"

"Hell, no, Jake! All I want is time for us to get caught up! Time to get our kids fed, maybe collect up some furs so they'll be warmer. That last creek had otters and they make a fine cap! Warm and waterproof both!"

I just looked at him. He held my eyes for a minute, then looked away.

"Gus, I don't know how many people would die because you stopped to catch an otter, but I figure one is too many. We're going on."

"What kind of a man are you?" he almost whispered. "You're going to kill people if you keep on this way!"

"I expect you're right, Gus. As to what kind I am, I'm about as desperate as a man can get."

I turned around and pointed back to where we'd come from. "Santa Anna's back there somewhere. I've seen what Mexican soldiers do when they catch people like us, and Santa Anna has already said that any fighting man will be executed on the spot. He might let the women and children go, but do you want to bet that he will?

"What if he decides that shooting or lancing the families he catches will cause the rest of us to pack up and leave Texas? Do you want your family to depend on Santa Anna's mercy?"

He looked down, then shook his head. "Captain, I wouldn't have your job for all the land in Texas!"

Captain, not Jake. I noticed.

"I didn't want it either, Gus," I said gently. "But Sam Houston and Ed Burleson said about the same thing to me that I just said to you, to get me to agree.

"Something else; Ed pointed out that I wouldn't have family along. That way, I wouldn't be tempted to do what you want, stop for a while so that people can rest up. Now, if you want my job you can have it, Captain Smith. But if you ain't quite ready for that, I suggest you and the other boys get up front and find us something to eat before dark."

They left, but that evening when we stopped, they moved to another fire to cook the porcupine they'd caught, which was all I could spare for them.

Jean-Louis and I got nothing but water. I tightened my belt and when I did, I noticed how my buckskins hung loose on me. For a moment, I wondered whether I could trim off some of that tanned hide and boil it soft enough to eat.

I decided I'd better not, but if we didn't find food soon, I might be desperate enough to try.

The next day, we crossed a ridge and down in the flats near the Brazos, I spotted San Felipe. We got there late that afternoon.

***

They brought out what they had, none too much because they'd had some rough times too.

I gnawed on a piece of jerked bear meat as I made the rounds. I never cared for it fresh, but salt-cured it tasted mighty fine and I wondered if the rest would be gone by the time I got back.

I had to caution some of the women to not feed the kids as much as they wanted, at least not at first. Feed a small amount of meat, with a little of the cornbread and honey to take the edge off, then a little more later on.

After I'd made my rounds, I went to meet with Mosely Baker, the man in command of the militia.

He was anxious for news, and I wished I had better to give him. But I told him what I knew.

"Houston ordered you folks to burn Gonzales? I have a hard time believing he would do that!"

"He did," I told him, my voice nearly cracking because I was so tired. I wanted in the worst way to get some sleep, but it would have to wait.

"You know Houston?"

"Known him since he was called Big Drunk. He was living with the Cherokees at the time and he never said what was bothering him, but something sure was stuck in his craw!"

"He's got a lot on his mind these days," I said, "so I just hope he can leave the whiskey alone until the army gets to Louisiana."

"It's that bad?" Baker asked, looking like he didn't want to believe me.

"It is. I reckon you heard what Santa Anna did at the Alamo. His army is back there somewhere and if he figured to feed his men on what he took from us, they're mighty hungry by now.

"I figure he's coming this way, which is why I'm bringing as many women and children and old folks with me as I could round up. There are others down south of here doing the same.

"Want to hear what they're calling what we're doing? It's the runaway scrape, and I reckon they're right. We're running away, sure enough, and as for scraping, we've been scraping the bottom of the barrel for enough to eat and wondering if we could eat the barrel."

"I saw a few of your folks. I got to say, some look like they'd have to stand twice in the same place if they wanted to cast a shadow," he said. "Hungry people are apt to get sick, so what about disease? Have you had sickness?"

"Chills and fever, so far, and before you ask, yeah, we've had deaths," I admitted. "People have been cold and hungry most of the way and I'm surprised we haven't had more,"

"We'll do what we can to help you," he said, "but we'll have to keep some for ourselves because I reckon we'll have to leave too. You're sure Houston ordered everybody to burn their homes and head east?"

"I am. Santa Anna's Mexicans might get the land, but they won't get what we've built. I can't speak for Sam, but I 'spect he's figuring that Santa Anna promised our property to his officers, especially the big cotton plantations east of here.

"They might have forgotten about the Indians, though. They ain't exactly fond of whites, but most of them purely hate Mexicans. They haven't forgot what the priests and soldiers did.

They made some into slaves and some of the ones that wouldn't accept the church, they hanged."

"I heard about that. As for Santa Anna, there's no telling what he might do," Baker said thoughtfully. "Sees himself as the new Napoleon. I've heard folks say that he plans on making himself emperor, and if he can push us out of Texas he might just do it.

"Think about it for a minute. The only thing between him and the American border is Texas. Over to the west is the Camino Real that runs through Paso del Norte all the way up to Santa Fe. From there, Mexico owns everything all the way to the Pacific and up north as far as the British and Russian settlements. That's a lot of country, and now that we've shown it can be done, he could plant colonies up that way and push the Indians aside."

Well, I'd never heard the like! But it made sense, put that way. From Central America all the way up to Alta California, and from the Pacific Ocean east as far as the Sabine!

And there was no telling how far north he could push before he ran into opposition. The Russian and British colonies on the Pacific coast were pretty small, from what I'd heard.

Off to the east, Americans had crossed the Mississippi and gone up the Missouri, but not many of them. And considering the trouble they were having with Indians, I had to wonder; would they fight to hold on to that country?

I didn't know. I reckoned that Santa Anna didn't either, but he might be willing to send his army that far north to find out.

Big chunk of land, that was, enough to be a sure-enough empire!

The next morning, after a good night's sleep, we loaded up what the people of San Felipe could spare and headed east again.

Behind us came more wagons, and behind them I could see the smoke rising. A lot of Texas history had been made in San Felipe. Newspapers had been published and schools opened. The Conventions of 1832 and 1833 had been held there. The Consultation of November 3rd last year had been held there, which made the town the capital of Texas.

The government had moved out since then, so maybe it wasn't

now.

But that smoke meant that historic or not, it was all going up in flames while I watched.

Chapter Thirteen

I was dog-tired, but I kept pushing on.

There were more deaths, but now they were almost all old people who'd reached their limits.

I'd been keeping an eye on two widows over the past two weeks. Both had lost husbands during the Bexar fighting and now, it seemed like they'd just given up. Day by day, they lost a little more weight and weakened a little bit more. I wanted to help, but there was nothing I could do.

Sibby Leonard was gaunt to the point of emaciation when she died, and Elizabeth Yocum was only a little better when she passed a week later. We buried them, I said a few words, no longer needing to read from the Bible because I'd said them so many times, and we rolled on.

I had no way of being sure of the date, but judging by what the plants were doing, I figured it had to be April. Shiny green leaves covered the trees and back in the shaded areas, small violets bloomed. Dewberries were already beginning to ripen and the larger, sweeter blackberries would follow soon after, as would wild plums.

I rode past the wagons on a horse that was as exhausted as I was, as we all were.

What if we paused long enough for people and animals to recover?

Up ahead was another stream, either a creek or bayou to be forded as soon as we crossed the next low ridge, or maybe a river. I had heard of the Navasota, but I couldn't be sure if this was it, and I wished that I knew more about this part of the republic. I figured it was too small to be the Neches, which I had crossed only five years ago.

Back then, I'd been scared stiff at the idea of being

responsible for two men who, looking back, had been better prepared than me. Now? Almost a hundred women and their kids, plus a couple of old men, looked to me to protect them, and a mighty weak reed I was for them to lean on.

I had tried my best, and failed; but maybe I could save the others.

I caught up to Jean-Louis and told him what I had in mind. He agreed that the people desperately needed to stop and rest, but worried that we were too close to safety to give up. Yet if Santa Anna was far enough behind us, it might be worth the risk.

We talked it over and decided that the only way to tell was to send scouts back along our back trail.

He picked Gus Smith and Thaddeus Jones, because they had the two best horses. "Ride back along our trail for about half a day, maybe a little longer, and find a place to lay up. If you spot Santa Anna's scouts, I'm depending on you to let us know how much time we've got. *Whatever happens*, one of you has to get back with the news."

"I understand, Lieutenant," Gus said grimly. "More'n likely it will be Thad here. Tell you the truth, I'm plumb tired of running away. If I can get Santa Anna in my rifle sights, I'll be thinking of my little Sally when I blow his head off."

I wanted to say something, but there was nothing to say, for I'd said what was needed two weeks back on the trail. This time, there had been a few early flowers to mark her little grave, white prickly-poppies at the head and purple verbena for the foot. The ones who'd died before her, we'd had no way of doing anything but giving the bodies decent burial and a cross to mark the grave before heading on.

"You want to borrow my rifle, Gus? I reckon it's got more reach and if you hit him, that .54 caliber ball will do more damage than your .40 caliber will."

"I'll take it, Captain, and thanks. If I don't make it back…"

"I'll see to your family, Gus."

He nodded and the two men gigged their tired horses into a lope, heading southwest.

I called Jean-Louis in closer, where the rest wouldn't

overhear. "I reckon I've killed too many of our people, Jean-Louis. I just can't face up to killing any more. Soon as we get across that river, I've made up my mind to camp behind the first big grove of trees and spend at least a day resting up.

"I figure there's more than enough game around to give everybody a good feed and I'll bet the youngsters can catch some fish, which will also help. There's plenty of grass for the animals—we fed the last of the corn from that abandoned farm two days ago—but grass this rank will put a little flesh on them.

"Your men need rest too, but we're still in Indian country, either the Wacos or maybe the Choctaws, so they're going to need to stay alert. Stand down half for a couple of hours, and after they've had a chance to rest, switch them for the others.

"I don't know exactly where one tribe's hunting grounds ends and the other one's starts, and maybe they don't know themselves, but they're apt to be touchy. This is prime hunting season for them, at least in this part of Texas. I hear they stock up after winter before they head toward the plains. Anyway, they're liable to be out prowling around and they'll steal horses anytime they can."

He nodded and went off to talk to his hunters.

**

Late that afternoon, five riders rode in on played-out horses.

The womenfolk still had half an elk left over from the day before, so they finished butchering it and stirred up the coals. By the time the meat was cooked enough to not wear out their teeth, there was cornbread from breakfast that they'd warmed in a Dutch oven. While they ate, they gave us what news they had.

"Santa Anna isn't following you, at least not yet. Sam Houston and his boys headed more to the south and Santa Anna's been on his trail since he left San Felipe. Yesterday, the fifteenth of April it was, he showed up at Harrisburg and burned us out. Might have been because he hadn't caught up to Sam, or he might have done it from pure meanness. I don't reckon it matters.

"Sam's men are fit to be tied because he won't let 'em fight, 'cept for a little skirmish now and then. For all I know, they may have run him out of camp by now. We figure the only way they're going to get away from that Mexican army is either swim or learn to fly, and they ain't got much time to learn how to do either one.

"A week from now, Santa Anna will own Texas, and he ain't taking prisoners. That's why we left. We've got family up near Nacogdoches and friends across the Sabine in Natchitoches. We figure to take our families across on the ferry and fort up on the other side, maybe shoot a few when they come up to the river."

"We heard about him not taking prisoners," I told him, "but as I remember, there's a big thicket between him and us. His army will have to turn around and circle back before they can come up to Nacogdoches. How much farther do you reckon before we get there?"

"Three days if you hurry, longer if you don't. We'd admire to travel with you if that's where you're going. And if you're willing to feed us, we'll do our share of what's needful."

"We can use the help, especially when we come up to the river," Jean-Louis admitted. But later on, after they'd gone off to set up their own camp he told me that he intended to have a quiet talk with his hunters and scouts.

"Jake, they may be just what they claim. But they might also be thieves or worse, so I'm going to have a few men watching to keep them honest."

I chuckled. "I had intended to mention that. Just because they're Texian doesn't mean they can be trusted!"

As it turned out, we had no trouble from the five and they worked as hard as any of us.

We rolled into Nacogdoches a week later. Others had come in before us, most from east of the Brazos, so the local folks were expecting us.

"Are there any more coming along behind you?" the former alcalde asked. He was still in charge, though nobody had figured out what to call him now that Santa Anna was coming. He hadn't fought against Mexico, but I figured he wasn't fool enough to think that Santa Anna would leave a Tejano in charge of the biggest town in this neck of the woods.

"Not that I know of," I said. "But there's more than one trail, so if they were north or south of us we might have missed them.

"If you folks can take care of our women and children, we propose to head south and see if Houston still has an army. If he does, we'll join up. Judging by what those men said, I reckon he needs every man he can get. We're experienced riders and we've all got rifles, so I expect he'll find a use for us."

"You're right, but you'd best hurry. You heard about him burning Harrisburg?"

"I heard," I confessed, "but to tell you the truth, I don't remember a town by that name. Is it over west of here?"

"Naw. It's down south, just before you get to Galveston. Not much of a town yet, but folks figured it might get to be as big as Galveston one day.

"There was talk of dredging Buffalo Bayou so ships could come farther inland, but I reckon if it happens now, Santa Anna will do it and only Mexican ships will get to land there. But we'll take care of your folks. How long before you intend to head down and look for Houston?"

"Tomorrow," I said.

***

I reckoned that I wasn't a captain and Jean-Louis wasn't a lieutenant any more, now that we'd got to where we were going.

But that didn't last long. Next morning, as soon as we saddled up to head south, the five who'd joined up from Harrisburg and another 26 from Nacogdoches and the farms around showed up. They'd heard we intended to join Houston, and since they were as stiff-necked as the rest of us, they figured to go along.

They even had a name picked out, the Nacogdoches Ranging Company, but they hadn't got around to electing leaders yet.

Gus Smith nominated me and since nobody else got nominated, I got the job. I nominated Jean-Louis as lieutenant and somebody growled back, "I'm plumb tired of waiting around. You two mind if we get going before it gets too dark to see?"

So we did.

Two days later, we met up with four men who claimed they'd been in a fight.

"Sam didn't want to, or said he didn't. But he told Deaf Smith to burn the bridge, which was the only way Santa Anna could retreat."

"Burned a bridge?" I asked.

"He did. President Burnet and the rest of the government had already headed for Galveston, figuring to take ship for New Orleans I reckon."

I just shook my head.

"How did Houston stay ahead of Santa Anna?"

"Had him a steamboat, he did. Called the Yellow Stone, it was, and Old Sam claimed that it won the battle for him. Now I hate to call him a liar, big as he his, but it was us that done the fighting while Sam was laying there on the ground."

"He was killed?" I asked, alarmed.

"Naw. He was bad wounded and he might yet lose his foot, but unless blood poisoning sets in I figure he'll make it. Anyway, Santa Anna, near as we could figure, had made up his mind to take all the seaports from Galveston to Linnville. Kick us out and not let us back in, we figured. After that, all he'd have to do is build presidios along the Sabine River and the Gulf to keep us from coming back.

"Burnet and the rest figured to get out while the getting was good and I didn't much blame them. It sure didn't look good at the time.

"We all figured Sam would cross into Louisiana, but instead he headed for Harrisburg. Could be he did it because for the first time, we had cannons of our own. Two six-pounders they are, called the Twin Sisters, that come down all the way from Ohio by ship. Colonel Neill it was that took charge of them. Good thing for us that he got out of the Alamo when he did, because he knowed all about cannons."

"This sounds like nobody was really in charge. And you really whipped Santa Anna's army?" I asked skeptically.

"We done 'er. They got used to chasing us and decided to take their reg'lar afternoon siesta. Didn't even have pickets out, so I reckon they were some surprised when they woke up and seen us coming! Whipped them fair, we did, and Colonel Hockley's cannons sure helped. Reckon they figured we didn't have any."

"Wait a minute; you said Colonel Neill was in command of the artillery!"

"Wal, he was, but before the main fight broke out he got wounded. Hit in the hip by part of a grapeshot, I heard, and it crippled him up so he couldn't keep going. General Burleson was sure upset when that happened. They'd been in more fights together than a body could shake a stick at!"

"Did you hang Santa Anna?" I asked, still confused and despite what the man had said, there were lingering doubts. I figured that if any man ever deserved hanging, it was him.

Ordering prisoners to be shot or bayoneted after they'd surrendered? And I also couldn't help remembering the women and children I'd said words over, because we couldn't stop long enough for them to rest or be fed a proper meal. If it had been my choice, I'd have strung him up and let him kick until the devil got ready to personally take him to hell.

"Nope. We looked for him after the battle, though to tell you the truth some of the boys were more interested in the silver those Mexican soldiers had. But he was nowhere to be found."

"So he got away? From a whole army?" I was astonished at the level of confusion that had existed. Was this man telling the truth? Had they fought against only a part of the Mexican army?

"Nope. He run like the rest of 'em, but we kept on looking. Caught him too, the next day it was. He had swapped that fancy uniform of his, but when one of his men called him El Presidente, we knowed who he was. We wanted to hang him, but Sam talked us out of it.

"Said if we hung him, they'd just find somebody else to raise another army and head north. The fighting might stop for a few months, but the war would just keep on going. And while it did, we couldn't head back home, those that still had one I mean. But we catched Santa Anna hisself and General de Cos too. They sure did have a bunch of generals, but in the end it didn't do 'em no good.

"The war was over, so I figured they didn't need me now and I've got to get a crop planted. It's already late April and if I don't get seed in the ground quick, I won't have no vittles come winter!"

Jacob Jennings

Chapter Fourteen

We were escorted into the camp by a pair of grim-looking men who took us to their new commander, a man named Mirabeau Lamar. The name sounded French, but he spoke American with a southeastern accent so I didn't have much trouble understanding him.

I figured Sam must have been short of colonels, because Colonel Lamar had joined up as a private. But I reckoned him to be a good hombre, because when the Mexicans had Tom Rusk surrounded he rode up with a cavalry detachment and chased them away.

I remembered Tom from the Gonzales fight, so I was glad he'd made it through the war. As for Lamar, even the Mexicans had saluted him for his bravery, so I guess he deserved to be a colonel.

I sure didn't want to be one! Being a captain was bad enough, and glad I was that the ranging company had split up as soon as we got to the battlefield.

Maybe they figured there was still silver in a few Mexican pockets and went off to search, although the bodies that were still unburied smelled pretty bad.

Lamar sent the same two hombres with Jean-Louis and me to see Ed Burleson, but when we got there he was asleep. "He's been up since the fight, seeing to things."

The speaker, a sergeant, was in charge of several men watching over the general to make sure he wasn't disturbed.

"Sam was bad hurt. There were some others too, so we had to get them back to the wagons. Some of the people that stayed back knew how to treat wounds. We had to make up a burial party too. Nine of our boys was killed, and I don't reckon anyone has tallied up how many of Santa Anna's soldiers won't make it back to

Mexico. But we caught 'em nappin' and licked their whole army. We captured more than 700 of them, and a bunch of muskets and pistols besides. Swords too, and a chest full of silver! Might have been more than one, now that I think on it. We also got their mules, horses, tents, everything they had."

"I reckon Ed's pretty busy, now that he's in charge, but when he wakes up I'd appreciate you telling him that Jacob Jennings and Jean-Louis Lafitte stopped by. Sam and him sent us up here with a wagon train of women and kids, so if you'd let him know that they're staying with families around Nacogdoches it might relieve his mind."

"I'll do that. Your horses look used up, if you don't mind my sayin' so. We've got all of Santa Anna's, so why don't you find Sion Bostick's cavalry detachment and tell him that I sent you to swap your horses for some of the ones we captured?"

"I remember him from the fight at Gonzales," I said. "Good man."

"You were in that one? I don't remember you, but I got there late and the fog was pretty thick. But now that I think on it, you do look familiar."

"I didn't last long," I confessed. "I got one shot off before my horse fell on me, and I don't remember much after that."

"That was you? I helped lift that hoss so you could be pulled out from under him!"

"I thank you, but like I said, I don't remember much about that day."

"I reckon you fixed up my rifle too! Ain't had a lick of trouble with it since, and I never did pay you! Tell you what, long as you don't mind Mexican silver, I'd admire to pay my debt now!"

By this time, Jean-Louis was grinning at my confusion. "You go ahead and pay him, and after that, I 'spect we ought to swap horses and be on our way. If you show up in Gonzales after we get back, I'd admire to buy you a drink!"

***

Our horses were mustangs, tough and able to do well on a diet of prairie grass. Or if that wasn't available, weeds, brush or even the tips of tree branches would do, but they'd come a long way and the grain we'd fed them to make up for not giving them time to graze had run out two weeks ago. We talked to Sion, then turned them in with the Mexican stock.

"I'll keep an eye on them. Might be that if they recover all right, I'll need new animals when we start back," he said.

"They'll serve you well," I told him. He nodded and rode slowly into the herd, edging some of the animals toward where we waited.

The geldings we chose looked to be blooded stock of some kind, possibly the personal mounts of senior Mexican officers, so I figured we got the best of the swap. We saddled up and shook hands with Sion, then headed out.

As soon as we were away from the camp, which we were glad to leave because of the stink, I gave Jean-Louis half of the silver that soldier had given me. Likely it was loot off of a corpse, which was why he was being so free with it. Or it could be that there was more than one of those chests of silver the sergeant had mentioned, and somehow the ones who'd found it forgot to tell anyone.

None of my business if they had, I figured. If they turned it in, that bunch of politicians who'd taken off instead of staying to fight would get it. Better that it went to whoever had found it.

People noticed those big horses when we rode into Nacogdoches. We turned them into the livery and asked that they be given a measure of grain if any was available. The stable-hand said there was and when we asked, he gave permission for us to bed down in his hayloft that night.

The trip had been long and we were tired, but not ready for sleep.

We found a tent that was selling beer and something they called whiskey, so we walked in and ordered a beer. If a man was aiming to get drunk, as more than one did, then that whiskey would likely do the job. But folks called it rot-gut for a reason.

We ordered a second beer after that first one and drank it slow, just looking around at the men leaning against the big plank that served as a bar. I spotted Fred Duty and nodded at him. He nodded back and walked over to us.

"I'd admire to buy you boys a drink," he said. "My wife told me you had a rough time of it."

I thanked him and confessed, "Rough enough. Next time I see Ed Burleson coming my way, I'm apt to turn around and start running!"

He chuckled. "Persuasive feller, Ed! Say, did you two just get to town?"

"We did," Jean-Louis said. "Just got back from down along the San Jacinto River. That's where the fighting was."

"I was there," Fred agreed. "Soon as the fighting ended, my neighbors and me headed up here to see about our families. Have you talked to Missus Sanders yet? She was some worried about her husband."

"She's right to," I said. "Reckon she's the widow Sanders now. Will was killed during the fighting around Bexar."

"Aw, hell! You're sure?"

"One of his neighbors was with him when he died. Shame, but a lot of good men fell. I hope Ed hangs Santa Anna!"

"He won't have to look far to find men to pull on the rope if he does. But Will's widow needs to know. She's poorly, from what I hear, and her daughter's worried."

"Priscilla?" I asked. He nodded, and told me where they were staying.

I asked Jean-Louis if he wanted to deliver the bad news, but he just shook his head. I didn't blame him; I would have shucked the job onto him if I hadn't of been the captain during that trip.

Libby Sanders was indeed poorly. She'd lost weight and a bright spot on her cheek was about the only color in her face. I said hello and asked about her, but she shrugged it off. "I'm dying, that's how I am! Have you heard from Will?"

"I'll see what I can find out," I said, trying not to lie, but not willing to add to her burden.

"Promise me you'll talk to Priscilla," she said, her voice showing how exhausted she was. "She's got things she needs to say."

"I will, Missus Sanders. Is there anything I can do for you?" I asked.

"You just take care of my little girl." She started coughing and held a rag over her mouth, and when she took it away I saw blood.

Not the first, either; there were dried flecks in several places, and I understood that consumption was killing her. Likely she would have lived longer had she been able to stay in Gonzales, but here in east Texas, with the heat and damp to get into her lungs?

Just one more mark against Santa Anna! A shame that he could only be hung once, for if a creature ever deserved to die several times, it was him!

After that, she sighed and drifted off to sleep. I walked out, as quiet as I could to keep from waking her, and Priscilla came out with me and closed the door softly.

"We have coffee, Jake. The neighbors have been very kind to us. Can I get you a cup?"

"I'd admire one, Priscilla," I replied.

We sat outside in the shade of a big pin-oak and sipped our coffee. "Your mother said you wanted to talk to me?"

She looked away, then turned to face me. "She told me I had been a young fool, and that I should apologize to you."

"I don't understand," I said, puzzled. "You've got nothing to apologize for."

"I do, and she told me that if I didn't I'd regret it all my days. She was right. Jake, can you forgive me?"

I just shook my head, not having an idea of what she was talking about. So I said so.

"It was what I did on the trail," she said, "when I sat with Jean-Louis. Jake, I like him, but I was just trying to get you to realize that I'm not a child! I'm a woman, Jacob Jennings, and you ignorant…"

I reckon if she'd been close enough, she'd have whacked me with that coffee cup. But I was safe, for a little while at least.

"I knew you were growing up, but Jean-Louis…he can do all the things I can't. He speaks French and Spanish and he can talk to anyone, but there are times I can't get started. He's also got a grant of land, while all I had was that forge and then the whole thing burned. I know, because I lit it myself to keep Santa Anna from getting it. I just…I couldn't see why you would look twice at me as long as you had him. But as for forgiving you for something I never understood, why, it's done.

"As for what your mother asked, I'll do my best to take care of you if you'll let me. Something I decided not to tell her…well, the truth is your father won't be coming. He was killed at Bexar. I figured it was wrong to not tell her, but I'll take the blame. I just couldn't make myself do it, seeing how sick she is."

"So you'll take care of me? Did you understand what she meant?"

"I reckon. She wants us to get married, doesn't she?" I asked. Saying it left me feeling all hollow. I felt like there was a great big hole in front and I'd just stuck my foot over it and was about to fall in. But she smiled, and things started looking better.

"She does. She knows how I feel, and that's why she told me I was a fool. But I won't hold you to your pledge unless you want it to happen. Do you?"

"More than anything," I said, and realized that it was so. "Priscilla, let's see about finding a priest. If you're willing, that is."

And suddenly I had two arms full of crying girl, or maybe she was laughing. I don't reckon it mattered. She never said yes exactly, but I figured if she'd meant no she'd gone about it the wrong way!

We sat there, not saying much. She snuggled in against me and I held her, and without noticing it at the time that hollow feeling went away.

A little later, we went in to see if her mother was awake, but I saw right away that she was never going to wake up. I reckon she hung on just long enough for me to show up, which was why she had a sort of half-smile on her face.

Or maybe, like folks say, she'd run into Will as soon as she passed.

I don't reckon it matters which.

Chapter Fifteen

Libby's death put thoughts of the marriage aside.

"Jake, I don't know what to do. We can't just bury her like we did the ones that died on the way!"

"I don't know the way of it here, but did she have visitors? Friends?" I asked.

"I should have thought of that," Priscilla said. "If you'll stay with her, I'll find Sharon. Her mother will know what to do."

"I'll stay," I said. "Who's Sharon, and why her mother?"

"I met Sharon right after we got here, and she's been my best friend ever since. Her mother is Evangeline Plummer, and her family has been in Texas since the beginning. She knows everybody, and women, especially the ones who came with us, look up to her."

She left, and I looked down at Libby. By the looks of things, she had died easy and it didn't look like she'd felt any pain. I brushed off a couple of flies—seems like they can sense death almost before it shows up—and covered her face with the bedsheet to keep them from coming back.

After I'd done what I could for her, I made a pot of fresh coffee, poured myself a cup, then went outside to wait.

By and by, a regular caravan of women walked down the lane and turned in. Up front was a woman I figured had to be Evangeline Plummer. Priscilla was following along behind the older ones and talking to a young woman, red-haired and pretty. Whatever they were talking about, there was a lot of hand-waving and low murmuring going on.

Evangeline shooed the two young ones my way and the others swept inside, several carrying bundles in their arms. They looked like they knowed what they were doing, so I sat there and kept my mouth shut. Being officially promised as I now was, I figured I'd have to get used to all kinds of woman stuff going on behind my back.

Priscilla poured coffee for herself and her friend, then sat down by me and introduced Sharon. I nodded politely, said howdy, and then asked what the others were up to.

"They're preparing my mother's body," Priscilla said, her voice catching for a moment. "One of the women donated a dress—they're going to burn the one she was wearing, and the bloody cloths she used when she coughed—and they contacted Mister Córdova. He said he'd see about having a coffin built and the grave dug. By tomorrow they'll have a carved cypress board ready to mark the grave."

"Who is this Mister Córdova?" I asked curiously. "Seems like he can get things done."

"He's the Alcalde, or was," Sharon explained, "but he's still in charge until the new government appoints a new one. They may not, because he was one of the original supporters of the Constitution of 1824."

Pretty, and knowledgeable too! Nearly as pretty as my Priscilla, I figured.

So we talked, and inside mysterious things went on. After a while, a donkey showed up pulling a small cart that was carrying the coffin. Evangeline came out and bossed the two men who'd walked alongside of the donkey as they carried the coffin inside.

It wasn't long after that before a small procession came along, led by a black-robed priest and another man. Jean-Louis followed along behind them, but we would have to wait to catch up on the happenings.

"That's the alcalde," Priscilla said. "I don't know who the priest is, but I'll find out because we'll have another job for him. I don't want us to get married today, but I don't want to wait any longer than we have to."

I just nodded back. Seemed like I was doing a lot of that lately.

Priscilla and Sharon went inside and I went over to make my manners to the two leaders. As soon as I did, the alcalde introduced himself and the priest. "I am Vicente Córdova, and this gentleman is Father Michael Muldoon. We are fortunate that he is visiting at this sad time.

"I regret that we have only a short time to speak, because I have heard many good things of you, Señor Jennings. We must arrange to meet again. It is unfortunate, but matters must proceed without delay. It is a hot day, and rain is expected soon. You understand?"

I did. Best to get it done before the body started to smell bad.

The same two who had carried the coffin inside came to the door and motioned to Jean-Louis and me to come help, so we did. The four of us carried the wooden box outside and carefully placed it on the cart. Then, with the priest leading and apparently praying, we started off for the cemetery that was about a mile away. Whatever he was saying, it wasn't American and it wasn't Spanish. Maybe it was that Latin I'd heard about.

Priscilla walked behind the cart, with me holding her hand, Jean-Louis and Sharon walked behind us, and behind them came Evangeline Plummer and the rest.

We ended up at a pretty spot, on a low hill that was surrounded by magnolia trees in full flower. Off to the side stood boards with writing on them that marked earlier graves.

Things had been a lot simpler back on the trail, but I figure that ceremony is important to folks. At least, this time I wouldn't be the one trying to find proper words to speak over the grave!

Father Muldoon said a final prayer, the men who'd dug the grave began filling it in, and most headed back for town just as the first sprinkles landed on us. Priscilla didn't seem in any hurry to leave, so the three of us stood with her until after the gravediggers had gone, then we turned her around and started for town ourselves.

She had held up well, but now it seemed like she had come to the end of her rope. I kind of knowed how she felt, because I'd felt that way too after I got back and found my family gone. There's an aloneness, a realization that the last person you could count on to always take your side wouldn't be there next time she was needed.

We took Priscilla back to the now-empty house, and while

Jean-Louis and Sharon waited under the porch with her, I made coffee.

After that, I held her while Jean-Louis and Sharon chatted and eventually she came around. It was like she'd just woke up from a sound sleep and hadn't quite figured out where she was. I reckon the mind can do funny things to hold off the worst of the grieving.

Late afternoon came on and we hadn't eaten since breakfast, so Sharon and Jean-Louis went in and fixed a simple meal. While we ate, we talked, and eventually the topic got around to us being promised to each other.

That put the cat among the pigeons for fair, at least among the two women. Jean-Louis looked spooked by the idea and I reckon I was too, but determined to go ahead with it if it killed me. Or at least killed my former plans to go back to Gonzales and start up my business again.

Jean-Louis walked Sharon back to her mother's house and Priscilla and me talked. Or rather, she plotted and I listened. For a minute I wondered what I'd let myself in for, then I figured out that it didn't matter. I had given my word, and a real man, or one who figures himself to be, won't go back on that.

Back when I was a boy, I had it easier than I knowed at the time!

"Did you notice how taken Jean-Louis and Sharon are with each other?" she asked. "Wouldn't it be nice if all four of us got married at the same time? I'm sure the priest would be happy to do that!"

I nodded, but a tiny suspicion was born. Was that what the two had been so talkative about, back when they were coming back with Sharon's mother? But while I was still untutored in the finer details of how women think, I wasn't dumb enough to open my big mouth and get myself in trouble! That could wait until after we were married, which I figured was the proper thing to do.

Turned out that the priest was too busy, him being some kind of negotiator between the Mexican government, Santa Anna's military, and the new Republic's government. Two days later, Ed Burleson showed up in town to talk to him, so we were put off again.

Jean-Louis and me had run out of things to say, and the women were off buying food, them still having some of the money Jean-Louis and me had given them. Good thing, too, because we barely had enough for a couple of mugs of beer. We headed for that tent saloon to spend it.

Turned out, we didn't need money. We ran into Gus Smith and four more who'd come with us on the Runaway Scrape, and they insisted on buying the beer!

Gus asked me what I proposed to do, now that Gonzales Town was nothing but a pile of ashes. I explained that some of my tools might have survived, but after thinking about it, I realized that the fire would have ruined them.

"I don't know what I'm going to do, Gus. Seeing as how we plan to be partners in whatever we do, we might go back to that land grant Jean-Louis had claimed."

"Is the grant still good, Jake?" Gus asked. I looked at Jean Louis and he looked at me and shrugged; neither one of us had an answer.

"I hear that veterans of the Revolution are entitled to a head-right, the same as what the Mexican government was handing out before the war," Gus offered. "You could each claim one. Take up farming or ranching, maybe. Or do some speculating in land."

Milt Fairleigh drained his mug and motioned for refills, then said, "They're only going to give that to men who were heads of households before San Jacinto. That means that to get the full allowance, a man had to be married before then. Single men only get a second-class headright, which ain't nearly as much the way I heard it."

We looked at each other, Jean-Louis and me. I didn't know what to say. Whatever plans I had just went flying out the back door. "I hate to say it, boys," I finally admitted, "but my business went up in smoke, along with the rest of Gonzales Town, and what with the revolution and the fighting I never got around to filing for a grant. I may have to take Priscilla back to the states and see if I can find a job back there."

"What, leave Texas?" Gus looked at me like I'd just sprouted

114

horns. "Jake, you can't do that!"

Jean-Louis looked equally flabbergasted, but I was thinking of the wife I would soon be responsible for.

"Jake, suppose we speculated in land using my grant?" he suggested. "I've got that league, what some are calling a sitio now, and we could try selling off parts of it. Like you said, we're partners. I figure we need to see what we can do right here before we give up on Texas."

"I don't see as that's enough, what with the condition of that land," I pointed out. "Some that I've seen is barely good enough to pasture a couple of milk cows!"

Gus drained his mug and signaled for another round. We finished our mugs and took a swallow or two from the new one. Was that the fourth or the fifth round? I couldn't remember, and I felt like laughing.

Shucks, losing my memory already and me still a pup!

"Jake, what if you and Jean-Louis could qualify for that first-class headright? You were both officers during the revolution, that ought to count for something! And neither one of you shirked his bounden duty like that bunch of politicians did! By thunder, you'll get that full headright if I have to tie Ed Burleson and Sam Houston both up until they do right by you!"

I reckoned that beer had more kick than I'd first thought. It was clear that I wasn't the only one whose prop-ups weren't too steady.

We jawed a while longer before heading back to the livery stable. We saw to our horses, then turned in for the night in the hayloft. I figured that Gus had been just blowing off steam. But now that I had time to think on it, there had been quite a few heads nodding. And maybe not because they'd been asleep, as I'd thought at the time.

We didn't know it, but the ones we'd left at the saloon weren't done yet.

Was that crazy idea Gus came up with drunk, crazy, or inspired? But after Ed Burleson told me about it, I knowed enough to keep my mouth shut so I don't reckon it matters.

***

After a certain amount of staggering, five former scouts who'd come to Nacogdoches with the wagon train located Ed Burleson. Red-faced and grinning, they offered him one of the mugs they swiped from the saloon before they left and told him that I had mentioned leaving Texas.

Ed, so they said later, was as shocked at the idea as they were.

"Now here's the thing, General," Gus said. "Them two were both elected officers during the trip here, and the next morning we elected them captain and lieutenant of the Nacogdoches Ranging Company."

Ed showed his amusement. "Okay, they were officers. I don't recall that company at San Jacinto, but I'm sure you had good intentions."

"We got there a tad late for the fighting, but we did help with the burying. But my question is, are you going to tell me that officers during the revolution are going to be treated like trash? Is all that free land going to go to the shirkers that never fired a shot?" Gus was clearly angered at the prospect.

"I hear what you're saying," Ed said, "but the law is clear. Only married men get the full sitio."

"Well, then! By grab, they wuz both married during that trip!" At this, even the woozy party that had come along to support Gus looked astonished.

Ed Burleson looked amused. "How do you figure that, Gus?" he asked.

"You know how things were when this was Mexican Texas and there weren't enough Catholic priests around? Folks just announced they were married and signed a paper saying they would do it all right and proper when they could find a priest?"

"I remember," Ed agreed. "And some decided later on that they'd made a mistake and just tossed that paper in the nearest fireplace. But you're going somewhere with this, so enlighten us."

"There was these two widow women on the train," Gus said. "Didn't have nobody to look after 'em, ain't that right, boys?"

The 'boys', none of whom had borne that title for at least twenty years, solemnly nodded. "You're talking about Missus

Yocum and Missus—I forget her name, but I know who you mean," one said.

"Yep, and I'm prepared to swear that I heard both of them talking while I was driving their wagon. Said Jake and Jean-Louis were just like their hus…ah, *first* husbands, the way they saw to their needs, they did."

There were looks of astonishment and respect as the others nodded their heads. Clearly, Gus was smarter than anyone had figured!

"And let me guess; neither of the 'wives' made it here, did they?" Ed asked.

"No, pore things," Gus struggled for a moment, then managed to look sorrowful. "The one passed on, and after she did the other one lasted only a few days before she died. But neither one were alone up to then, and after they died we buried them proper and put up crosses before we moved on."

"So let me get this straight," Ed said, now smiling. "You're willing to swear that both were married before the March deadline, and therefore entitled to full first-class headrights?"

The nods were unanimous.

"One final question, Gus," Ed asked. Do Jake and Jean-Louis know they were married?"

"They will by the next time you see them, General!"

Chapter Sixteen

"Jake, that woman just won't let up!"

"Which one, Jean-Louis? Priscilla or Sharon?" I asked.

"Priscilla! But she's thick as thieves with Sharon, and between the two of them I can't figure out whether I'm coming or going!"

I laughed and he glowered at me. But I noticed that he hadn't run away. If he was really all that afeared, all he'd have had to do was saddle up and go.

So I listened to his complaints, then talked about how one sitio of land wasn't much to start a speculating business. I mentioned that we'd had several offers to buy his Mexican grant, but we hadn't sold because if we did he'd no longer have the makings of a horse ranch. And if he kept it, we could always go back to Gonzales and maybe rebuild, me as a blacksmith and gunsmith, him as a trapper, breaker, and dealer in mustangs.

"Course, I wouldn't have many customers, and it's not much of a place to take Priscilla, what with no women there to talk to. I reckon she'd be lonesome, not to mention that would leave Sharon alone back here. A body can't tell *what* might happen, the way the Indians are acting."

I gave a nudge now and then, but he talked himself into it. The upshot was that we did what the women wanted and had a joint wedding, with the women smiling and us looking scared. After Muldoon had us sign his book, he beamed at us and sent us on our way. Charged us four silver dollars, too!

But after it was done, we looked up Ed Burleson to thank him and to ask his advice. A knowing man, Ed Burleson; he'd been in Texas a long time.

"I believe I'd take a look down south of Gonzales," he said. "Most was claimed, but many a good man fell during the Goliad fighting and some didn't have family to leave their claims to. They escheated to the Republic, meaning that the land is available."

I didn't know what that meant, but Sam, being a lawyer, did, and he explained it so I filed that word away in my memory. One day, I might need it to impress folks!

Another place he suggested was near the Pedernales river, and if that was already claimed, look at Johnson creek. Rivers were prone to flooding, which spring-fed creeks usually weren't, and as for bringing ships up from the Gulf, not many rivers were deep enough or wide enough, so we might have to forget that idea.

The four of us talked it over. Jean-Louis and me had planned on being partners anyway, and our wives being friends just made things easier.

One other thing Ed had suggested, sell off Jean-Louis's grant so that we'd have starting capital. We looked around and soon found ourselves a lawyer who would handle matters. Frontier or not, there was no shortage of lawyers in Texas!

My lot in Gonzales was likely gone, although a man could always go out to the edge of town and stake out another if he was a mind to. Texas was never going to run short of land, though some might not be all that good.

As for that Llano-Estacado grassland out west of Austin, I couldn't see why anyone would ever want it. The Comanches wanted it for buffalo country, which was about the best use anyone could make of it. Let them have it, I figured, if that would keep them from raiding farmers and ranchers east of there!

So we talked, and made sort-of plans.

The women wanted us to settle close to each other and neither of us minded that. But being as we weren't close to a settlement, the wives might need to fight off a raid.

Jean-Louis claimed he was a better shot than me, but I knowed better. So both of us worked on teaching the women to shoot their new rifles. I taught Sharon, he taught Priscilla. The arrangement kept the arguments down some, but never quite stopped them.

The other thing we needed to do was get them good mounts, the best we could find.

We talked about taking a trip to Mexico, but after thinking it over, buying good horses didn't make much sense if a feller got killed in the doing. The Mexicans were still touchy, because of losing the war the way they did, so while the two of us had only been in one fight, they weren't likely to see a difference between us and Sam Houston himself!

We now had money and we were anxious to find new headrights that we could lay claim to, so one Thursday morning, with a freedman and his wife that we'd hired as wagon driver and camp cook, we headed south.

It looked like Galveston would soon have competition, for there were already work crews surveying and dredging Buffalo Bayou. Two brothers named Borden were surveying a townsite that took in Harrisburg, the town Santa Anna's army had burned.

We went through around noon and didn't slow down. It was so hot that we had sweated through our clothes and the mosquitos were everywhere, but we found a nice creek with a sandy bottom and banks to camp by. The mosquitos were behind us and I, for one, hoped they stayed back there.

We got an early start the next day and found the road leading to Hogan's Ferry on the Brazos, which we crossed the next afternoon. By then, the land had begun to change, less boggy and with fewer of the giant southern live oaks that are found close to the Gulf. But we camped under one, and between its wide-spreading branches and our canvas tents, Priscilla and me stayed mostly dry during the downpour that night. Not so with Sharon and Jean-Louis, who swore they'd nearly drowned!

Try as we could the next morning, we couldn't get the soggy oak branches to burn, so after handing out some of our jerky, we went on.

The Guadalupe River turned out not to have two adjoining parcels, but over twenty miles to the east of Victoria was a pleasant little stream named Garcitas Creek. We explored it and found another creek that was lined with willows. Not far from where the two joined, we found the places we wanted.

Claiming our headrights turned out to be easy. The clerk promised to search through earlier claims, but he thought that the two sitios, originally part of De León's colony, had reverted back.

The brothers who'd owned them had died at Goliad.

As for the headrights, he came out personally to confirm that we had them.

"I never saw anything like this, but according to what a friend in Austin sent me, Sam Houston and Ed Burleson both attested to your claim!"

"I was in the Gonzales fight with Ed," I explained, "and later on, I met Sam. We both did, so it's nice that he didn't forget us now that he's President."

"Well, he didn't, so I filed your claims. Anything else I can do for you?"

There wasn't, so he headed back.

***

Victoria was an easy day's ride away.

Jim Fannin's Texians had come here from Goliad in 1836, but after the Battle of Coleto Creek, the town had been occupied by Mexican soldiers. Whether because of that or because it had originally been part of De León's mostly-Mexican colony, the residents had been Mexican or Tejano.

We visited the town, talked to businessmen and generally made ourselves known, and our wives found friends among the women.

I mentioned that I had been a gunsmith in Gonzales and when I mentioned opening a similar business in Victoria, the people I talked to thought that was a good idea.

But Jean-Louis and me both felt that my gunsmithing business should wait until after we'd built homes on the headrights we'd claimed, because winter would soon arrive.

***

The land was generally flat, with wide fields of tall grass that could be cut for hay. There were also occasional clumps of trees, and when the wind came from the south we could smell salty air coming up from Lavaca Bay. We figured that when storms blew in, a few trees for windbreaks would be mighty nice, so we kept that in mind when selecting our locations.

I also wanted direct access to Garcitas Creek, which I figured would be useful. Sooner or later, ships would come to Lavaca Bay and with them would come trade. The ship wouldn't be able to sail up the creek, but a boat could.

Turned out we didn't have to look far for help. As soon as we told people what we intended, men started showing up.

Some of them were men who'd fought at San Jacinto; others were Tejanos who had no home to go back to. The ones with the most common sense became our foremen, which took some of the burden off us.

There were disagreements now and then, sometimes between the Anglo veterans and the Tejanos, but the foremen dealt with them, usually by firing the one who wouldn't listen to reason.

I remembered that Tejano militia captain who'd come up from Victoria when men started showing up from other settlements to help, and he wasn't the only one. Austin had appointed Juan Seguín a captain, and his Tejano company had fought at San Antonio and at San Jacinto, He'd also accepted the surrender of San Antonio's Mexican garrison when it left there for Mexico.

He was as much a Texian as anyone, to my way of thinking.

We told the foremen what we wanted, they offered suggestions from time to time, and then saw to getting it done.

***

The next few months were busy, despite the occasional norther that swept in starting in November. But by then we had sturdy cabins of logs for ourselves and bunkhouses for our workers. We hunkered down and stoked up the fires until the storms blew out, then went back to work.

Jean-Louis figured to resume gathering and selling mustangs in the spring, but we decided that we'd also breed the best ones in an effort to develop better stock. The Mexican horses we'd gotten had impressed us, and we figured if they could do it, we could too. I thought to do the same thing with cows later on.

Meantime, Jean-Louis would need hay for his animals and I made up my mind to supply it. Let him use his land for pasturage; I would cut hay on mine.

We talked it over in April. I was anxious to open an expanded gun-related business, where I could do sales, repairs, and conversions of older models. We decided that rather than her staying out at the ranch and me going home on weekends, we would live in town and leave the running of the rancho to a manager and his wife.

One other influence on our decision: Priscilla was pregnant, and when her time came she would want other women around.

We found out a month later that Sharon was pregnant too, but by then she and Jean-Louis had a comfortable house of adobe and people to help. They would live on the rancho, but there would be visiting back and forth between us.

By May, what with all the building and hiring, we had about run out of money.

I negotiated a loan from a man named Brownson, who with a partner named Goldman had a store not far away. They figured I was a good risk, and after I got my business going, they wanted me to help them when they got around to opening a store in Victoria. They were hesitant about doing that right now, because so many Tejanos and Mexicans had left after the Revolution that Victoria's population had declined. A general store that served only a few customers wouldn't prosper.

The reason for the population decline? Fearing for their lives, the Mexican people who originally settled Guadalupe Victoria had fled across the Rio Grande to Mexico.

They had reason to be afraid.

During the Revolution, General Urrea had reluctantly followed Santa Anna's orders to execute men who'd been captured in the battles that had taken place near Victoria. Also executed was Colonel James Fannin's Goliad command, who'd surrendered after being promised treatment as prisoners of war.

Urrea had fought in uniform and done what he could to oppose the executions, but for Carlos de la Garza and the local rancheros who'd served as Urrea's irregular scouts, there would be no forgiveness.

Texans had committed their share of atrocities too, which mattered not a whit to the newcomers who'd come to Victoria after San Jacinto. They had first refused to do business with the

Mexicans, and later on there had been reprisals. As a result, many had abandoned their homes in Victoria and fled to Mexico.

I thought of how we'd burned our homes and run away from Santa Anna's Army. Down here, the people hadn't burned theirs, but they'd run away from the returning Texicans.

Which was why excellent properties in newly-renamed Victoria were now for sale cheap.

I thought about how it seemed wrong of me to do it, but if I didn't buy one of those nice houses someone else would. So I did, using the money that Brownson and Goldman had loaned me.

I figured I got the best of the swap, and maybe that's how it works when your army wins.

***

The new year of 1837 opened to a succession of storms. First had come a norther, and as it blew out there had come the Gulf storms, one after the other.

The barrier islands offshore stopped the huge waves, but not the wind, which howled around the buildings even as it brought moisture to dry fields.

I figured we were fortunate, because we had shelter, firewood, and dry hay in the barns for our livestock, not that we had all that many yet. There was still plenty of grass, but there would be no more cutting until the land dried up.

From time to time, we heard news from Houston, the new town that had sprung up north of Galveston.

Sam had tried to make peace with as many tribes as he could, and most had agreed, but the Comanches had refused.

The government insisted they had the right to send people into Comanchería, but the Comanches wouldn't allow it; they figured that after the ranging companies had come and gone, settlers would follow, and they had no intention of surrendering more of their territory.

The ranging companies went in, and soon after that, there were raids on outlying ranches and forts. Men had been killed, as had some of the women; others, along with children who were old enough to ride, had been taken captive.

Infants had either been abandoned to die or murdered outright.

***

Gus Smith showed up one day. I hadn't seen him for more
than a year, and I was surprised to learn that he had settled on his
own sitio north of Jean-Louis's. We talked business for a while—
he wanted a plains rifle like the one I'd loaned him—and I
promised to either find him a Hawken or make him one myself. I
invited him to dinner and after a friendly drink at the saloon, we
headed for the house. Priscilla now had a Mexican woman who
served as housekeeper and on occasion, cook, so I didn't anticipate
a problem.

We settled down after dinner with a bottle of good French
brandy I'd bought from a smuggler. He'd spoken to a fisherman
who'd passed the message along to me, and I'd gone down with a
wagon and bought the brandy, as well as all the coffee and tobacco
he had. Indians were now growing tobacco, but most preferred the
smuggled product, claiming it was of better quality. I didn't care,
because I'd stopped using it.

Gunpowder and smoking is a bad mix.

Now Gus and me sat sipping that brandy and he told me of his
concerns. "I'm out there by myself most of the time, just me and
my dogs. They'll let me know if any Indians come sneaking
around, but being as I'm only one man and not as spry as I was,
knowing ain't likely to do me much good."

"What about your family, Gus?" I asked.

"My wife died of a stomach ailment of some kind and the girls
were taken in by her sister. They're doing fine and I get a letter
every few months, but living with me ain't suitable. And to tell the
truth, I ain't fit company for a female now."

"Sorry to hear that, Gus," I said. "You mentioned dogs; how
many do you have?"

"Only about thirty now, half of 'em bear-dogs, the rest coon-
dogs. I lost two when they tied into a big old bear, but one of the
bitches is gonna have puppies any day. I hate losing a bear dog, but
I couldn't do without my coon dogs."

I raised my eyebrows at him, so he went on. "I've got a strip
of land along the Lavaca River that's planted in corn and coons.

I've got a bunch of bee trees too, but I only raid them once a year and I don't take everything."

"Corn and coons?" I couldn't help but grin at that.

"Yep. Some of the corn is for feed and I use the rest to make whiskey. I sweeten the mash with honey, seeing as it's free and sugar ain't. The coons come in to eat my corn, so I trap 'em and sell the skins. The meat I feed to my dogs.

I've also got a bunch of hogs down in the river bottom and I shoot one now and again. A pair of them rooted their way out of my pen and hid out down there about two years ago, and now there's more'n a body can eat!

"Some I keep for myself, the rest I either salt-cure or honey-cure, before finishing it in my smokehouse. Right tasty, it is, and selling it brings in a few dollars for whatever else I need.

"Tell you what, next time I'm in town I'll bring you a few jugs of my whiskey. It ain't as smooth as this brandy, but it does warm a man. And maybe a smoked ham or two?"

So I said that would be right nice of him, and next day he went on his way.

I found out later that some wouldn't buy his smoked meat unless they were sure it was pig. A few were suspicious that when he hadn't killed a pig recently, Gus smoked a few of the coons he'd trapped and sold their meat as pork.

Chapter Seventeen

Spring turned into summer, and it didn't take long for my new business to bring in more work than a body could do by himself. I hired a man who claimed to be a gunsmith, then another one who was.

Folks were nervous. There was a lot of this and that going on down in Mexico. If things kept on the way they were going, I figured it was only a matter of time before the war started up again.

I talked it over with Jean-Louis and he agreed. From that day on, we had a wagon ready-packed and parked in the barn. I might not make it out of Victoria, but as soon as the baby was born I intended for Priscilla to move to Ten Springs Rancho, what I'd named my grant. If I got cut off in town, Jean-Louis would try to get our families to safety.

Mexico wasn't all that far from Victoria. By sea, a ship leaving Matamoros had an easy voyage to Matagorda Bay where an army and its supplies could be offloaded. By land, it was longer, but if the army crossed at Laredo and headed northeast it was less than 200 miles by road.

Nervous Texians brought in their rifles to have me replace springs that were perfectly good, and do a little filing here and there to make them feel better to the shooter. I also converted old flintlocks to caplocks and sold the owners more caps than a body would need any time soon, but it might be that they figured to practice.

Most had hard money, usually Mexican silver. Politicians were scheming on both sides of the border, but reasonable folks figured that business was business. If a Mexican trader had something you could sell at a profit, it only made sense to buy it. It went the other way too. I was glad to get the money.

Jean-Louis was selling horses too, and as soon as he could afford it he used that money to buy good Mexican breeding stock.

Once a month, sometimes more often, we all got together so the women could gossip about having babies and what-not while Jean-Louis and me talked business.

***

One day, a man came in with something I'd never seen before.

I held it and it seemed to fit my hand. The long barrel was steady when I pointed it at a hook I'd mounted on the wall, but that fat round thing in the middle was like no pistol I'd seen before.

"What do you call this?" I asked him.

"That's a Colt's Revolving Pistol," the man said. "He calls it the holster model and I reckon that makes sense, seeing as how it won't fit a pocket. It ain't all that easy to load, being as you have to pop out that barrel wedge to start, and a feller has to be careful doing it. As soon as you've done that and slid the barrel forward, you can take out the cylinder, that part you mentioned, and reload it. Put 'er all back together, stick the wedge back in, and you're ready to cock the hammer and shoot. It can hold five loads, though most figure it's better to keep one chamber empty. But if a body was expectin' trouble, the thing to do would be load all five."

"I've seen twister pistols and this looks kind of like one of those, but it's lighter! Pepperboxes, too. What would you take for this one?"

"It's not for sale," he said, which I figured meant he was going to get as much from me as he could.

Meanwhile, I had removed the caps, cocked it and let the hammer down, my thumb holding on to make sure it didn't damage the nipple. I watched what happened when I cocked it and noticed a small piece of iron slide into a cutout on the cylinder. Smart, I figured, to lock the chamber in line with the barrel that way.

He wanted more than I was willing to pay, so I didn't buy it, but he told me that the factory was in Paterson, New Jersey. I straightened the bent trigger and filed it smooth to keep it from hanging up, which was why he'd come in in the first place, and handed it back.

I made up my mind to write to Colt and ask how much he'd

charge me for some of his pistols. But then I thought that maybe I could shorten the time that would take; it was said during my sailing days that if a body had the money, he could buy anything he wanted in New Orleans.

I hadn't heard of my uncle Henry for more than a year, but a letter addressed to him in Galveston would reach him in as little as two weeks. I penned the letter, and a chore it was, then sent it off.

The next day, after I'd thought on it, I wrote another letter, this one to Samuel Colt, asking how much he would charge to ship me two dozen of his pistols. After that, I put it out of my mind. He might not write, and if he did I might not have enough silver to pay him what he wanted.

I forgot about it in the excitement of what happened next. A young woman who was servant to the family that lived near our house came running in and told me Priscilla had gone into labor. I took off my apron and shrugged into my coat, then grabbed my hat and cane. The sword-cane might not be needed, but times were still unsettled and I hadn't taken to carrying a pocket pepperbox as some did. I didn't trust the things, being as it was apt to freeze up when a feller needed it most, and until then it was heavy and awkward. Gamblers kept one in a pocket, but they did their work sitting down.

Time I got there, my son Edward Samuel Jennings was squalling like a catamount and waving his little fists around. The two women there with Priscilla, who looked plumb tuckered out, told me how much he looked like me, but I figured if I looked that ugly then Priscilla wouldn't have married me. But it made them happy, so I just nodded.

***

It was more than a month later that I got Sam Colt's letter. He'd crossed out more lines writing it than I had writing mine to him, but I could read it.

He thanked me, offered me a job if I was a master gunsmith, and explained that they were hard to come by back there in New Jersey. Men who could operate his machines were fairly plentiful, but those who could do the careful filing and polishing and fitting that was needed during final assembly were as hard to find as hairs on a frog!

As for cost, the .36 caliber pistols, the kind people living on the frontier wanted, weren't available. In fact, despite the Army rejecting them for use as a service pistol, there was a waiting list that he proposed to fill eventually. He'd added my name and in a year or two I could expect one that would have the improvements he was already planning to make.

But he did have a few non-working holster models that had been sent back for defects. He offered me a box of them and mentioned that the frames and cylinders were in good shape, but some of the smaller parts had failed or been lost. He couldn't afford to take gunsmiths from production jobs, but if I wanted the parts, I could probably make as many as 15 working versions from the 25 that didn't.

And he wanted half price for his collection of junk, only $625.

I thanked him for his confidence, but pointed out that I might not be able to make even *one* working version, not knowing what he proposed to sell me. But if he was interested, I might pay $250 for his box of junk. That's what I called it, and referred him to my uncle Henry as the agent who would pay him and transport the box to Texas.

I also sent a letter with the particulars to my uncle, which took more time than it should have. I was busy learning a new trade, waking up in the middle of the night and handing Little Ed to his mama to do what I couldn't.

I figured that if I had been born properly equipped for the job, she'd have made me feed him too, as well as change his nappies, which smelled worse than a roomful of dogs with dyspepsia.

It was close to six months later that a rider showed up to tell me that the *Eureka* had come in to Linn's Landing on Lavaca Bay. My uncle had the box Colt had sold him and wanted me to come pick it up. He also wanted to talk to me.

I hadn't seen him since I left the ship in 1835, so I made up my mind to take Priscilla and Little Ed down to Lavaca Bay if she felt up to it.

Garcitas Creek being a tad higher than normal, I figured to

take my 24-foot boat and just float downstream, which would be easier on her than riding in a wagon.

It was equipped for rowing, having two sets of oarlocks, but we wouldn't need to do more than keep her between the banks. While I was there, I might see if *Eureka's* carpenter could make me a mast-step and a mast and boom. The sailmaker could fit it up with a suit of sails and I already knew the way of setting up standing rigging to support a mast, as well as running rigging to handle the mains'l and a scrap of jib.

That way, I would be fixed to trade with folks who sailed in after dark and figured to be gone before daylight.

***

Uncle Henry's hair had turned gray and he had a fair crop of wrinkles I didn't remember, but he was still pretty spry. He and the bosun rigged a hoist for Priscilla and Little Ed that soon had them on board, despite the racket when the bosun's chair spun around a time or two. Priscilla shrieked, Little Ed squalled, and if Uncle Henry hadn't of scowled at the crew they'd have been laughing at the commotion.

But by and by, we were in Uncle Henry's cabin, at least for a while. Little Ed had done what came natural to him while on the way up, so Uncle Henry and me were glad to wait on deck and smell the sea-breeze while she changed his nappy and washed off the worst of the damage.

And complained that she'd been offered as much sea-water as she needed, but when she'd insisted on drinking water it had been mighty scarce for the task.

Uncle Henry had thoughtfully brought the brandy and two glasses with us as we went on deck. While we sipped, he explained why he'd wanted to talk.

"Jacob, I'm of an age when the sea no longer calls to me as it once did. I'm of a mind to go ashore and take up farming, as did my father and my brothers."

I was surprised at that and wondered what it had to do with me, except for a kind of general telling. But I kept quiet and just nodded like I understood.

"I have in mind a small farm," he said, "perhaps 360 acres,

where I can build a house and raise a family. You have a son to carry on your name, but I have none and it's time I did something about that. I have money put by, so I expect finding a wife to be as easy as sailing down-wind."

"I reckon I understand. Do you have a farm in mind?" I asked.

"Not yet. But I'm hoping that you would be willing to take the Eureka in exchange for 360 acres of good bottom-land. I've asked around and since you're not doing any real farming, that land along the creek is not being used."

"I'm not interested in going to sea, Uncle. I have my business on shore and my family to think of. As for the land, you mentioned that you had money. I wouldn't mind selling you land for your farm and helping you to get started."

"I expected that would be the way of it, you not going to sea, but what if you were a land-based absentee owner? I've two good seamen who would sail Eureka for you on shares. Texas is starting to boom and bottoms are few for the trade that's already ongoing, so I expect they would do well.

"Set up a warehouse on shore, perhaps hard by Linn's Landing, and make that your home port. Have them call at Guadalupe Bay for cargoes coming and going to Victoria, from there to Copano Bay, then around to Corpus Christi Bay and by longboat, up the river to San Antonio de Bexar! You'll have no problem shipping a full cargo from there, and then it's east to that new town of Houston on Buffalo Bayou! Since you're trading only within the Republic, there would be none of the duties on your cargo that you'd be responsible for if you traded with New Orleans."

Well, he talked me into it. We offloaded Sam Colt's junk-box and went back on board my boat, which now had a mast with a gaff-mains'l and jib that attached to a small jib-boom the bosun had added without my telling him.

He was one of the pair who'd sail Eureka on shares, so he wanted to stay on my good side!

Chapter Eighteen

We had promised to help my uncle Henry get settled, but Sharon's time had come and Jean-Louis was as nervous as a cat in the middle of a pack of dogs.

She had Priscilla to help, and after a while she came out and told Jean-Louis that he was the father of a daughter. We celebrated in good old Texas style, which made both our wives mad as wet hens. But by the following afternoon we were mostly recovered, and they soon got over it too.

The place Henry had picked out for his house was all wrong. It was too close to a low-lying area, meaning that Mosquitos would swarm in the summer, and if the creek flooded it would be under water.

After we told him what we'd noticed, he went with us and together we picked a nice spot farther upstream that was on top of a low bluff with a steep slope leading down to the creek. The Indians likely wouldn't raid this far south, but if they did the creek and that bluff on one side would make fighting them off easier. Comanches being horse Indians, they couldn't ride right up to the house on that side.

Then we got started on his house.

The people who'd built our haciendas knew the way of adobe and they all had friends and relatives that needed work, so a day or two later the place looked like a beehive! People were coming and going, some I knew but some I was sure I'd never seen before, and all were busy on one thing or another. There was a lot of talking and laughing going on down along the creek and the sounds of axes and two-man saws never seemed to stop.

Both of our foremen had come over to help organize things, and after they talked to us we agreed to what they had in mind. Some of the new workers would stay on to work for Henry, the others would go back to what they'd been doing on my place or

Jean-Louis's.

Most of our employees were dark-skinned, and some were darker than that.

As long as a man did his work without shirking and got along with the others, neither of us cared what his last name was. That's the way of sailors, and we figured if it served when one man could kill a bunch of others by not doing his share, it would work just as well on shore.

The wives fussed a little at first, not being used to it the way we were, but the nannies having names like Vargas and Rodriguez got them over that. Our employees seemed to be satisfied to work for folks that thought as we did. Now and again we met with our foremen to see if there were things we ought to know about, but it was always "No, señor! 'sta bien!" Even so, we kept our eyes open because a man can't afford to be careless when his family's life might depend on his alertness.

Every month, we made it a practice to get both crews together of a Saturday afternoon for a meal. Now and then, we bought a couple of pigs from Gus and had him deliver them on the hoof to either Jean-Louis's place or mine. The next time, I'd have a word with my foreman and he'd round up a wild cow for the feast. Easy enough to do, because there were hundreds of them running loose along the creek, and all of them long-horned and bad-tempered.

We also brought in a barrel of beer, and depended on the foremen not to let the drinking get out of hand. Nobody ever quit us, far as I know, but some who didn't measure up got fired.

Time to time, with all the mixing, I wondered which one of us they figured they worked for. One week, you'd see a vaquero on my Ten Springs Rancho working wild cows out of the brush, the next week he might show up at Jean-Louis's South Plains Rancho to help with breaking mustangs.

But since we were partners, I figured it didn't matter none.

Priscilla and Sharon, between mothering chores, got together once a week or so and decided how much money we had. More than enough, I figured, since both women now had store-bought dresses that they wore to town, and when they went outdoors put on hats that had come from far-away places like New York.

It might have taken the hats two years to make their way down to New Orleans, then over to Galveston, and from there on the *Eureka* to Garcitas Cove, but most of the time they were still in good shape when they got to my place. Priscilla would send someone to let Sharon know when a shipment arrived so that they got first pick. The rest were sold to women in Victoria, which likely brought in enough profit to pay for those dresses!

My gun business was booming, so much so that I didn't have time to work on that box of pistol parts. But by and by things slowed down, and I looked at what Sam Colt had sent.

He should ought to have been more careful, the way I saw it.

After I got through counting the parts, I figured that by making replacements for the busted or missing parts myself, I had enough for at least twenty-four revolving pistols. There was also a set of drawings he'd sent along, of a proposed change that would make loading easier.

Maybe that was why he'd sent me as much as he had; the old parts wouldn't work with the new models.

I sorted things out and soon figured that the cylinders, along with the breech and arbor, were the most critical parts. I might be able to make them from stock if I had to, but it would be a lot of work and take considerable time.

With all the new work that box represented, I understood right off that I would need good help. It came to me that instead of looking for journeyman gunsmiths, I might be better off with a pair of apprentices.

So I looked around and found two young men who'd come down from San Antonio, needing work.

They were ragged and looked like they'd missed more than one meal, but they stood up straight and looked me in the eye when I talked to them. Good enough to start with, I figured.

Turned out that they were cousins, orphaned during the cholera epidemic that had come to San Antonio before the Revolution.

That was a bad year for the cholera, but at least things out here hadn't been as bad as they'd been in Galveston. Folks there had also suffered from measles, yellow fever, and smallpox at one time or another.

The boys were glad to get the work, and now that Priscilla was out at the hacienda raising Little Ed there was plenty of room to give Jeff Bell and Milt Harris their own rooms.

I insisted that they work as hard as I did and be careful in the quality of what they made, but I remembered what it had been like for me at their age. I tried to treat them like my uncle Henry had treated me, and it wasn't long before they were more like members of the family than apprentices.

***

That summer, and on through the winter, the news that came to us was a mix of good and bad.

The older Comanche peace-chiefs had kept things under control while Houston was in charge, but even back then it didn't do to feel like they were friendly. Being split into different bands the way they were, and with horse-stealing viewed as a test of manhood, there were bound to be misunderstandings.

A skilled thief would be in and gone before anyone knew he was about, but their youngsters had to learn the way of things just like ours did. Some did, but some never got the chance, because settlers that caught one were apt to hang the horse thief if they didn't shoot him first. More often than not, that resulted in an Indian raid or two before things settled down.

One of the raids had hit Parker's Fort a few years back. Matters might have been worse had Jim Parker, who'd been working in a field about a mile away, not seen what was happening and got there in time to hide 17 people.

But several men had been killed, and the Comanches took three women and two boys with them when they skedaddled. One of the women had since been ransomed, but no one knew what had happened to the others.

Not for lack of trying, though; Jim Parker had gone into Indian country three times since then to try to find his nephew John, but each time he had come back disappointed.

After that, I reckon he gave up. The boy was either dead or

had been adopted into the tribe, and by then he was apt to be as much Comanche as Texian.

Vicente Córdova, who'd been so helpful after Priscilla's mother died, had gathered a mixed group of Tejanos and Cherokees that eventually grew to around 400; they had decided to support the Mexican Constitution of 1824 instead of the Republic. Their uprising didn't get very far—General Tom Rusk had called out the Nacogdoches militia—but feelings were still running high over in the east.

Córdova had somehow slipped away, so there was no telling what he might do next.

But those things were a long way off, hundreds of miles from our ranchos. More worrisome to us, Santa Anna was back in Mexico and nobody was sure if we'd seen the last of him. He was mostly being quiet right now, but nobody expected that to last.

I figured we were going to need those revolving pistols, so I got to work on them.

***

Time I was done, they weren't Sam Colt's version but at the same time they weren't my work either. My pair worked as well as that first one I'd seen, and Jean-Louis also had two. Our wives, being less likely to need a pistol, each had one. Henry had one too, and Milton and Jeff, being as they'd done a lot of the work, had one apiece.

I tried hanging a holster on my hip from a belt, but it banged around so much that I figured it was more trouble than it was worth. Besides, nobody in Victoria wore a pistol unless he was looking for trouble. Like as not, somebody would stick a knife in him and steal the pistol if he did.

But as horse pistols, they worked fine.

Both Jean-Louis and me had found that we liked California-style Mexican saddles with mochilas. The saddles were easy to make and if a vaquero broke one, as sometimes happened when he roped one of those big longhorned bulls, they were easy to fix. Replace that big Mexican-style horn if that was what was needed, or if the frame was cracked replace it and then transfer the horn to the new pommel. Then take the mochila from the old saddle, which had cutouts for the pommel and cantle, and fit it around the new frame.

It covered more of the horse than an American saddle did, which could be important when a man was bucking south Texas brush.

Adding a pair of holsters to the mochila's front flaps was easy, and since most already had pockets sewed, it got so that whenever we went anywhere on horseback those revolving pistols went right along with us.

Dismounting to practice and mounting up afterward was fairly easy; a man just had to be a mite careful not to snag his clothes on the pistols.

But the holsters were designed to make them convenient to a *mounted* man's hands, which meant that reaching up from the ground to grip the handles, then drawing that long barrel out of the holster, was a bother.

Jean-Louis practiced drawing the pistols first, then swinging a leg over the horn and dropping to the ground with them ready in his hands. Instead, I drew the off-side pistol, then dismounted with my left hand on the horn to steady me a mite.

My way didn't look nearly as showy as his, but I also never had a horse run off like happened to him twice.

I decided to have another try at making a belt and holster. A wide belt, say, and hang the holster lower so your elbow didn't hit it? And for walking, a thong to tie around the leg so it wouldn't bang around? And if on horseback, just untie the thong and let the holster hang down.

I talked to Jean-Louis's harness-maker and he allowed that he could have one ready in a day or two, but being saddle leather I would need to wear it until it fit. I nodded and said I would.

Neither of us were brave enough to try shooting from horseback, but one of the bronc riders volunteered to give it a try. He even managed to hang onto that pistol when the horse went to sunfishing, hand up out of the way until it had quit bucking.

Later on vaqueros took to holding their empty hands up like that so they'd be ready as soon as they could afford a revolving pistol of their own.

Horses never did take to the smell of powder smoke, and they purely hated the boom close to their ears, but the riders took that as a challenge.

A couple of months later, we had a dozen mounts that shrugged off the noise and smell like they were nothing unusual.

Some were deaf by then, I figured.

Sharon heard that another of the Parker Fort captives had been ransomed, a woman named Rachel who was distantly related through her marriage to Luther Plummer.

We didn't find out until later how they'd mistreated her and the baby she'd been pregnant with when she was captured, until she wrote about it. After people read what they'd done to her and her baby, nobody was much in favor of making peace with the Comanches.

When Rachel finally got back to be with her husband in February, she was covered by scars from them burning her to make her work harder. But they tried to make a go of their marriage, despite what had happened, and she had a baby the next January.

She died in March, which most figured had to do with what they had done to her. The baby died two days later. After that, more than one spoke of a war against the Indians and I had more gun repair business than I could handle.

But I remembered who'd helped me out before, and sent one of the revolving pistols to Ed Burleson as a gift.

Whether we ended up fighting the Comanches or the Mexicans, I figured that he'd find a use for it.

Chapter Nineteen

Victoria being the biggest town around, folks just naturally showed up when they needed things done that they couldn't do themselves.

I worked on their guns and while I did, they brought me news from other parts of the Republic. Sam Houston was about to step down from being president, but I figured he wouldn't just go off and hide.

Mirabeau Lamar, the vice president, was all set to take the office.

I remembered him from San Jacinto and I'd heard more of him later. Complicated man, Lamar. About the best-educated man in the Republic, some thought. He'd published a newspaper, wrote poetry, was a philosopher, whatever that was, and in a fight brave as a man could be.

But after David Burnet put him in charge of the Army, the men figured they had the right to elect their own general. So he quit the army and got himself elected Vice President. Always on the go, it was said, never wanting to stay still.

But after being elected vice president, he spent much of his time away from Texas. He considered Sam Houston's policy of seeking peace with the Indians appeasement. It was said of him that "he hated Indians and he hated Sam Houston, not necessarily in that order."

***

A messenger showed up one day with a note to let me know that *Eureka* was anchored in Lavaca Bay. I'd already been thinking about her for a while.

In the usual way of things, my factor in Linnville received her cargo, saw to temporary storage in John Linn's warehouse, and over the next few weeks, sold what wasn't intended for merchants in Linnville or Victoria on to San Antonio, Gonzales, and places that didn't have names yet. I'd gotten to depend on that income, but lately it had been less than I expected.

I talked to my uncle Henry about it, wondering if the men I'd hired to sail the ship were to be trusted. But after he explained, I understood what was likely happening. *Eureka* was old; her spars, rigging, sails, and even the hull itself needed near-constant upkeep. If she was to remain afloat, it was time to overhaul her.

"I had a letter last month from Captain Matthews," Henry said. "A voyage that took eight or nine days back when you sailed as crew now takes a full two weeks and sometimes more.

"She needs a careening to scrape off the weeds and barnacles, but to do that you've got to strip her down to the hull and lay her on her side on shore. I don't recall us doing that while you were crew, so likely you need an explanation of what's involved. The sails will have to come off her to start with, and it only makes sense to have the sailmaker make a new set while you've got the chance. Her sticks will have to come out, and more'n likely when you do you'll find a lot of the standing rigging needs replacing. After that, the cargo has to be offloaded, everything, right down to the ballast, before the crew tows her ashore and lays her on her side.

"I wouldn't be surprised to find that she'll need a few new planks as well as a re-caulking, and it might even be that a few frame members have gone rotten.

"She won't last forever, Jacob, but if you take care to see to her needs in a timely way, why, she could be sailing these bays a century from now! Captain Matthews was my bosun when I had her, and a good man he is. If there's aught needing to be done, he'll know.

"A word of advice, nephew; done right, Eureka is good for ten, maybe twenty years before she'll need another rebuild. Done wrong, she could sink in the next storm."

I promised I'd keep it in mind, and so long as Matthews could pay for what he needed out of ship profits I would be satisfied. In any case, I would need to hear what he had to say, so it was time for us to have a talk.

A fast trip down, meet with Matthews and also have a talk with John Linn. He'd built a wharf that would make unloading easier, but if he wanted too much for *Eureka* using it I reckoned Matthews could keep on anchoring out in Lavaca Bay and transferring *Eureka's* cargoes by longboat.

I figured to be gone three, four days at the most. The ride would do me good, seeing as I was spending most of my time working in my shop or talking to visitors.

Then Priscilla stuck her oar into the doin's.

"You can't leave before Thursday, Jake! You're not going without me, and Sharon will want to come too. We'll need the nannies for the babies, so make sure there's room in the cutter for everyone. And our trunks, of course!"

So much for my fast business trip. Now that the women had took command, there was no telling how long I'd be away!

***

I'd met John Linn a time or two before, but just to say howdy to. I figured we'd see more of each other, now that he'd just been elected mayor of Victoria, but it hadn't worked out that way. He spent at least as much time taking care of his business down in Linnville as he did in Victoria.

Linn got along well with Tejanos and Mexicans, who called him Juan Linn, which I saw as being in his favor. Mayors and businessmen ought to get along with everybody.

John was a businessman and a good one, which was why I'd recently commissioned my own warehouse in Linnville. He was a touch *too* good, I figured, which would last as long as he had a monopoly on Lavaca Bay's seaborne trade!

I'd thought to catch him in Linnville, but I missed him again; he'd just gone back to Victoria. Except for that, my trip went well and as for the women, I was just glad I'd been too busy to tell them what I thought of the dresses and hats that were being sold in the new millinery store.

A man ought to stay as far away from doin's like that as he can. Otherwise, he's just bound to get himself in trouble.

There was no tide to speak of when we set out the next

morning, but we caught a good onshore wind that took us almost all the way up Garcitas Creek. After it shifted, we rowed the rest of the way and as soon as we came in sight of the landing, people started heading for the dock to help unload.

Getting everything on shore was easy nowadays.

We'd built the dock first, and after that I'd described what I wanted to Martín, one of my workmen. He had sunk the bottom-ends of two big cypress logs alongside the dock, as deep into the sandy bottom as he could manage, with them leaning so that the tops crossed about 20 feet up. I'd forged the iron straps that fastened them together myself, and with the help of a couple of hands, climbed up and bolted everything in place. I'd done that job myself too, them not wanting to work that high up. Sailors knew the contraption as jeers.

After checking to make sure the link was solid, I hung a double-block from it, using a chain that I'd forged myself. Jean-Louis had showed up about then and decided to get in on the fun. Working together, the two of us ran a line through the king-block, then through the snatch-block that lubbers called a falling-block because pulling on the lines made it go up and down, and finished the jeers by feeding the line back up through the double-block's second pulley.

That block-and-tackle rig made lifting even heavy bales and boxes simple. Two men could now handle loading and unloading, one to haul on the line, the other to reach out, hook on to the bale or the falling-block, and haul it onto the dock as the lifting-line was lowered.

Jean-Louis and me had worked hard on everything we'd done, but I can't remember us ever being happier than when we were working on that jeers. It didn't hurt that the wives, who were expecting again, were smiling at our antics.

Life was good, better than I'd ever hoped for, and likely better than Jean-Louis had hoped for.

The Republic was growing, we were growing along with it, and there was no limit in sight. Seemed like every week or so another dozen families settled somewhere not too far away, and most of the menfolk had rifles. They'd come to take up the free land the Republic was offering, but they'd fight if it came to that.

Mexico's Centrists were still fussing about how the revolution had turned out, but I figured the longer they waited the less likely they were to try another invasion. Besides, they had other problems.

***

The Federalists, now calling themselves the Republic of the Rio Grande, had never stopped supporting the Constitution of 1824.

Texas had succeeded in separating from Mexico, so they figured they could too. The Republic might even join in on their side; after all, it was just across the Rio Grande!

They'd called a convention at Laredo and elected officers, including Jesus de Cárdenas as president, and declared independence.

For their territory, they claimed part or all of the northern areas of Tamaulipas, Coahuila, Nueva Leon, Zacatecas, Durango, Chihuahua, and Nuevo México.

But their insurrection, unlike ours, hadn't lasted very long.

General Mariano Arista caught up to their army and whipped them easily. The remnants skedaddled across the Rio Grande, them that still could, and some ended up in San Antonio.

Cárdenas and the government had made it to Victoria and didn't seem disposed to go any further.

They tried to talk President Lamar into supporting them, but he was more interested in making a lasting peace with Mexico. Might have worked, except that they weren't interested in making peace with us.

Hadn't stopped the insurrectionists, though. They were reorganizing what was left of their army and rearming it, with muskets imported through Linnville.

As for Santa Anna, who'd started the whole mess by abandoning the Constitution, he had got himself into another war. He'd barely escaped being hung after San Jacinto, but his time he hadn't got away clean. Fighting the French had cost him a leg.

After I heard that, I figured we'd seen the last of him.

Trade across the border, some of it even legal, was back to what it had been before the war. Mexican traders didn't want another war any more than we did.

***

Up north, things were different. The men I talked to were worried, and some of their concern had to do with President Lamar.

He was against allowing the United States to annex the Republic, which I didn't care about, but during the campaign he'd talked about Texas expanding all the way to the Pacific. That sounded good to me, though where he expected to find the cannons and soldiers and such he would need wasn't clear. We were lucky, having access to hard money from Mexico, because what the rest of the state was using wasn't worth hardly anything.

Lamar had another problem: the Comanches.

He also had a solution, one that was different from what Houston had tried: extermination, or at least expulsion. He'd sent ranging companies into Comanchería, which had stirred up the Comanches. They had struck back by raiding settlements. The result had been more men killed, more women and children taken captive, and stock stolen.

And then had come Rachel Plummer's book. It had been published in Houston, and while most hadn't read it, everybody talked about it.

She'd described what the Comanche women had done to her and how one of the warriors had murdered her baby. Not expressly detailed, but clear to everyone who knew anything about the Comanches, she had been ravished, and likely more than once.

But having just fought a war, and nearly lost it except for Mexican carelessness, people were tired of the fighting. Folks just wanted to get on with their lives.

Things had been mostly peaceful while Houston was president, so maybe they could be again. But first, the Comanches would have to return the captives—all of them—and stop raiding white settlements.

It seemed too good to be true when Muk-wa-ruh, peace-chief of the Penateka Comanches, offered to meet with the Texians in

San Antonio and talk peace. We didn't know it at the time, but smallpox had broken out a number of times among the Comanches, as had cholera. Weakened by disease and the ongoing war with the Texians, they had been unable to prevent other Indians from raiding deep into Comanche territory. Caught between the Arapaho and Cheyenne tribes to the north, the Apaches to the west, and an intractable Mirabeau Lamar to the east, Penateka Peace Chief Muk-wa-ruh wanted nothing more than to make peace with the Texians if he could.

That was the situation that prompted three Comanche chiefs to ride to San Antonio and ask for a meeting with Ranger Captain Henry Karnes. There had been a council, they said, and they wanted peace with the Texians, and they'd brought an Anglo boy as a sign of their sincerity.

Karnes was blunt; there would be no peace until all the captives were freed.

The emissaries said they would be. A delegation of chiefs would return in about three weeks with the prisoners and sign a treaty with the Texians.

Lamar was equally blunt; there could be peace, but only if the Comanches returned all their captives, agreed to stop raiding white settlements, and not interfere with Ranger companies who entered Comanchería. So another message was sent, asking for confirmation: the Comanches would return all their prisoners?

The return message said that yes, that was the agreement. The captives would all be returned.

A truce was declared so that the meeting could take place.

The agreed-upon date: March 19th, 1840.

Chapter Twenty

Thirty-three Penatekas, twelve of them chiefs, the others respected warriors whose words carried weight in Comanche councils, rode in to San Antonio. Some also brought their wives and children. Altogether, a total of sixty-five Comanches came in to the parley, most of them painted and dressed in their best. Chief Muk-wa-rah, second-ranking chief of the Peneteka Comanches, was their spokesman.

Among the ones that hadn't come were Buffalo Hump, a Penateka war chief, and Peta Nokona, chief of the Nokonis.

Buffalo Hump had never agreed to giving up the Penateka's captives. Mexican traders would ransom them, the Texians would too. He would not willingly give up his only source of money, for to do so meant that he couldn't buy better arms for his warriors.

The need was great, because the Texians not only had long-range rifles, their Rangers now had fast-firing revolvers.

Peta Nokona had his own reasons. He and Cynthia Ann Parker, taken captive during the raid on Fort Parker, had fallen in love and married. It was a match that would last the rest of their lives.

To return all the captives held by his band meant he would have to hand over his family to the hated Texans.

There to meet with the chiefs were Quartermaster-General William Cooke, Adjutant General Hugh McLeod, District Judge John Hemphill, District Attorney John D. Morris, and Bexar County Sheriff Joseph Hood. There was also an interpreter; none of the commissioners spoke Comanche and the chiefs spoke no English.

Instead of the expected 200 captives, Muk-wa-ruh's delegation brought only one, a 16-year-old white girl named Matilda Lockhart.

She had been horribly tortured, with burn-scars over most of her body, and her nose had been burned off so that the bone showed. She could not hold up her head, but she could describe what had been done to her.

She had also learned enough Comanche to tell the commissioners that Muk-wa-ruh had never intended bringing in even the thirteen captives his tribe held.

Instead, he planned to offer them one at a time for as much ransom as he could get. Spanish and Mexican negotiators had paid well to get their people back, the Texians would too.

What he did not understand was that the old ways were gone for good.

President Lamar had given strict orders that if the chiefs did not produce the captives as promised, they themselves were to be taken hostage for their return. To enforce this, three companies of soldiers, totaling more than 175 men, had been dispatched to the meeting.

The interpreter, when pressed, delivered the news to the chiefs and knowing what would happen, escaped out the door.

Colonel Fisher, commander of the First Regiment of the Texas Army, immediately ordered one company into the Casa Reales, as the courthouse was known, while two others remained outside. In the general melee that ensued, the chiefs were stabbed or shot to death, and in the dimness and confusion soldier's bullets also struck Texian attendees. The Comanches who'd been listening outside the Casa Reales tried to escape, but all were hunted down and killed or captured.

The Comanches were not the only casualties. Seven Texians were killed, including Sheriff Hood, and eight were wounded, three seriously.

After the fight, an elderly widow of one of the chiefs was released and told to inform the tribe that a twelve-day truce was in effect. The tribes could bring in the captives without fear of being attacked, but if not, the Comanche prisoners would be killed.

Instead, they tortured thirteen of the captives to death. Three others had been adopted into the tribe and so were spared.

Among the killed was Matilda Lockhart's six-year-old sister.

A rider headed to Gonzales with the news, and two days later we heard about it.

I figured it was only a matter of time before the Comanches retaliated. Priscilla and Little Ed were in Victoria, so I figured they were safe. It would take a powerful lot of Comanches to attack a town this size!

But Jean-Louis and Sharon were at his rancho and they would need to be warned.

Milton was the best rider, but I asked anyway. "I need one of you to warn Jean-Louis."

I waited, and sure enough Milton said he would go. "Tell him that Sharon and the baby can stay with us, we've got plenty of room. If he balks, remind him that his hacienda has thick walls, but walls only work if there's a man with a gun to keep the savages out."

Milton nodded and went off to the livery stable. We had taken to keeping half a dozen of our best horses there and he'd pick the one with the most speed and bottom; even so, the trip would take him the rest of the day.

"Jeff, I want you in the house with Priscilla and Little Ed until this is over. I don't expect them to raid Victoria, but a body never knows what might happen. You've already got your pistol, but take a couple of the others too. You'll also want a double-barreled shotgun in case they get close, and a rifle in case they don't. Take one of the kegs of powder and all of the molded bullets, and a couple of the lead bars too."

He nodded soberly, face stiff. I knowed what he was feeling. I was scared too, though a man doesn't show it.

"What about you, Jake?" he asked.

"I'll be along directly, bur first, I intend to find out if the militia needs anything. If they need me to join them, I will. You take care of my family, and if the Comanches hold off for a day or two, I'll send Milton to help. Tell Priscilla I've messaged Jean-Louis to scnd his family in, so she should expect visitors."

He nodded and started gathering up what he'd need.

While he did, I took down that pistol belt that I'd avoided

wearing up to now. I strapped it on, adjusted it to fit snug around my waist, and fiddled with the holster.

It hung from the belt by a three-inch wide loop, and it occurred to me that hanging it on my left side made sense. So I slid it around and tried that, with the butt sticking out forward. It still felt loose and floppy, but maybe…

I punched a pair of holes near the holster bottom and inserted the ends of a rawhide pigging string, then tied them around my thigh. No more bouncing or flopping around, and I could carry my rifle in my right hand without it banging into the pistol!

But if the Indians did come, I would need all five cylinders, so I loaded the empty one and fitted a percussion cap over the nipple. I gently squeezed the copper skirt to hold it in position and let the hammer down gently so that it lay between two of the caps. Not as safe as an empty cylinder, but there are times when safety comes in second.

My rifle was loaded, but I figured a fresh powder charge and a new cap would be more reliable.

I used the worm on the end of my ramrod to draw the bullet, which left it misshapen, so I put it in with some others I'd rejected to be melted down later. The powder I dumped outside, to mix with the dirt.

Before reloading, I put that cap back on the nipple and fired it. I figured if there was any of that old powder still stuck in there, that cap might set it off. But nothing happened, other than the pop of the cap, so I ran the nipple pick through the hole to make sure there was no fouling and reloaded.

I got a few stares during my walk down the street. The rifle in my right hand was unusual, but that pistol on my left hip was a sure-enough attention-getter.

But the ones who'd heard about the Council House fight understood, and nobody asked me fool questions.

***

I found John Linn in his office.

"What's the state of our militia, Captain?" I asked.

"Plácido Benavedez is the captain, not me," he said, "and the boys will fight, if that's what you're asking. You think the Comanches will come here?"

"I do not," I said, "but it don't do to be guided by wishful thinking. They're notional, and right now I 'spect they're as mad as hornets." He nodded understanding. Hornets were fierce when their nest was disturbed!

"Is that one of Colt's Paterson pistols?" he asked.

"It is, mostly. He was backed up when I wrote to him, so he couldn't sell me a pistol, but he did have a box of parts and he sold me those. I made this one from what he sent, and several others besides."

"Do you have any left?" he asked.

"Four or five, I reckon. You interested?"

"I am."

I started out asking what Colt charged for his, but let him talk me down to $40. I figured I might need a favor later on, him being the mayor, so it didn't do to make him mad at me.

We talked about the militia after that, and agreed that it was time to call them in and make sure they were ready. We talked more after that, but this time about me. He perked up when I mentioned what I'd done during the war.

"Jake, there are some new men in town that haven't volunteered to join the militia. I suspect it's because no one has asked them to.

"I'm prepared to appoint you captain if you're willing to raise a company from them. I suggest you talk to them, see what they think of the idea and mention that the Comanches might already be on their way. If they turn you down, you let me know. We don't have room for shirkers in Victoria."

"John, they'll want to elect their own captain," I pointed out.

"They may," he said. "But if they decide on someone I don't approve of, they'll find out that I'm not a man to trifle with. You've got the experience and you're the one willing to raise a company, which none of them have offered to do, so you'll be their captain or I'll know the reason why!"

I figured that was good enough, not that I was anxious for the job.

But we might need that company by and by, so getting them organized was worth the aggravation. We parted on good terms, John and me, and after he paid me the $40 I handed him my pistol.

There were others in the shop, so all I'd need to do was stop in and pick one up. And if somehow the boys had taken all of them, there were the two that I kept with my horse tack.

***

Jean-Louis and Sharon showed up with little Angie and her nanny. They would stay with us in Victoria, but Jean-Louis intended to head back for his rancho.

"Jake, I can't just go off and leave my men, and yours will wonder why you aren't there with them. The Comanches will raid places like ours, being they're a ways from help, but they won't dare attack Victoria. They won't like you abandoning them."

"Jean-Louis, my place is with our families. You're most likely right about them not trying to raid Victoria, but Comanches don't think the way we do and they're plumb riled up by what happened in San Antonio so I wouldn't put it past them.

"But if they do come, I intend to make sure they don't all get back home. Plenty of room in their happy hunting grounds, the way I figure, and I'll be more'n happy to send them on their way!"

"Put that way, it makes sense, Jake. What would you say to me stopping by your place and see how many of your men want to join me and my boys? The worst that will happen if nobody's there when they come is that they burn your house and the barn. We'd lose all our stored hay, but summer's coming on and we can cut more before fall. If they say no, I'll still do my best to talk your housekeeper and the cook into joining us, but if the men decide to stay I reckon that's up to them."

"My place is closer to town," I said. "You could have your people move in with mine."

"I've got a herd rounded up that I intended to drive down to Linnville, and if they don't show up right away, I'll go ahead and do that. But if I hear that they're coming before I'm ready, I'll have to decide whether to leave them in the pasture or scatter them out. They might just take the herd and leave. I hate to lose the work they represent, but…"

"I know what you mean," I said. "Well, you do what you think best. If they *do* show up, don't think about trying to out-ride them. Just get your people into the hacienda and fort up until they leave. Most are still armed with lances and bows and arrows, but not even a rifle bullet will punch through those adobe walls!

"I think you should let them take the horses. Ain't like there's a shortage of mustangs in Texas and we can always round up more to replace what they steal."

***

March turned into April, then May.

Little by little, folks decided that the Comanches weren't coming after all. They were still nervous, but the militiamen had farms and businesses to attend to and their families were showing the strain too. They had no liking for being shut up in Victoria with folks they weren't too fond of, and every old biddy had one or two that she felt that way about.

Jean-Louis and Gus rode into town one day, and we talked.

"They'll come," said Gus, "just as soon as they figure out who the chief is. More than one young buck will want to go a-raiding right away, but if he does, he'll have to talk the others into going with him all by himself. Judging by what I heard, most all of their big men were killed in that Council House fight, so they'll need to sit around the fire and jaw awhile.

"But sooner or later, they'll decide that one has better medicine than the rest. He'll be the new chief and after that, depending on how he feels, they'll either go back to raiding right away or they'll try to talk that ranger captain into another peace council."

"Any idea how long that will take, Gus?" I asked.

"Nope. Might be a day or two, might take a month or two.

"But they'll come. They figure they got betrayed, them having come in during a truce. They won't just let that go."

I wished that he was wrong, but I was afraid he was right.

Both of Victoria's militia companies had gone from being ready to fight to not being ready for much of anything except sitting around and bragging, but I had got used to wearing that heavy pistol on my hip. I made up my mind to keep on wearing it.

Five shots. Two for the savages. But if they kept on a-coming, I figured to use one on Priscilla and the next one on Little Ed.

The last one I'd use on myself.

Chapter Twenty-one

Later on that summer, we heard from traders of a few raids on isolated farms where horses had been stolen but it appeared that for the most part, the Comanches had learned their lesson.

But along with the other news, they mentioned that a small group of Mexicans had been sighted near one of the Comanche villages. John Linn opined that they were likely not aware they had crossed into Texas, but he asked to be notified as soon as possible if it happened again. We agreed that the government should be notified too, so that a company or two of rangers should be dispatched to chivvy them back across the border.

The unusual thing about that sighting was that except for a few bold traders who were well-known to the Comanches, Mexicans generally tried to avoid them as much as possible. But John didn't figure it was important at the time, and neither did I.

***

Early in July, I got a letter from Captain Matthews, who'd decided to sail *Eureka* back to Galveston for the careening. His reasoning, that the stores of rope and canvas and tar he would need were not available in Linnville, made sense to me, so I'd told him to go ahead.

In the letter he said that the careening was nearly finished.

He'd found out during the scraping that a few planks needed replacing, but the hull's frames were sound. The caulking would take a few days longer, but after that the hull would be refloated. Loading the ballast and the scrubbed-out and refilled hogsheads of water would take another day, but as soon as that was finished he intended to use the longboat to tow *Eureka* into Galveston, where there was a hoist he could use to emplace the lower masts. Once they were secured in place by the shrouds and stays, the lower masts themselves would support the upper sections as they were hoisted into position and secured.

The process was complicated and time-consuming, but at the same time commonplace. Ships facing major storms at sea not only reduced sail to ride out a blow, they sent down the topmasts and sometimes even the middle-masts. Doing so reduced the rolling that could overturn a ship and send her to the bottom.

He expected to finish sometime in late July, and after tensioning the new rigging to account for stretching, he intended to load cargo in Galveston and sail to Linnville. He expected to arrive around the first of August and suggested I might want to meet him there to go over his statement of expenses.

Jean-Louis had held on to his herd of mustangs, and now that the danger was over, he thought we should drive them to Linnville where he expected to find buyers. He suggested that the women take the cutter and asked me to bring some of my hands and help with the drive.

Broken to ride the mustangs might be; wild at heart they still were, and apt to take off at any time unless the herders were watchful. I agreed to bring enough men to help, because they represented more than four months of hard work. Our finances were in reasonably good shape, but losing a herd that big would hurt.

Herding the horses along would take longer, so we figured to head out two days early. The foreman would take over after we got there so that Jean-Louis and me could catch up to our families.

After an early breakfast the next morning, the point rider gigged his horse and tugged on the rope of a docile old mare.

She followed him down the road, and one by one, the herd walked over and fell in behind.

I was on the left flank with my men, one in front and two behind me, keeping them bunched. Jean-Louis and three of his were on the right, while the drag riders came up behind and pushed the laggards along. There were always some that wanted just one more mouthful of grass, but within a few minutes, they had sorted themselves out and the herd was on the move.

***

I had noticed during the times I was away that Milton was apt to take life easy while Jeff kept on working. Suspecting that he would do it again, I had a quiet talk with Jeff before I left.

"I expect the work to go on as if I was right there, and I expect you to see it happens. If Milton gives you trouble, you let me know when I get back."

"He won't sass me, Jake. I've whopped him before and I can do it again if needful. It's not that he's lazy or a bad worker, it's just that he can find a dozen things to think about. He'll lay down what he was working on and go work on something else. Flighty, you might say, but it's not all that bad. Lots of times he'll figure out a better way of doing something. But I'll watch him close this time."

I nodded, and as I rode off to join Jean-Louis, I realized that it wouldn't be long before Jeff was ready to open a shop of his own, maybe in Linnville where, last I'd heard, there was no gun-shop.

***

Two days passed without incident.

On the morning of the third, Milton quietly laid down the disassembled shotgun he'd been working on and walked over to where their pistols lay on the end of the bench. Jeff glanced at him, but said nothing until Milton walked toward him with one of the pistols slightly extended, butt first.

"What in tarnation do you think you're doing!" Jeff hissed.

"Grab your possibles bag, Cousin. I just spotted an Indian sneaking into the livery corral and if he's not a Comanche, I'll eat him feathers and all."

Jeff nodded and took the pistol. He quietly closed the front door to the shop, then hung his powder horn and leather bag over his shoulders before picking up his rifle.

No words were needed. Jeff kept watch through a loophole while Milton loaded the empty fifth chamber and stuck the pistol into his belt. Finished with his preparations, he took down his rifle and kept watch while Jeff followed suit.

"I don't see him right now, but he's there," Milton said.

"We need to warn folks," Jeff said, "because it's likely he didn't come by himself."

"The shot when I fetch the one I spotted will do as well as

157

any," Milton said. "I'll just slip over and do for him, and while I'm about it I want you to head over to Judge Garfield's house and wait for me by the southwest corner. I 'spect I'll be running when I head back and it just might be that a Comanche or two will be on my heels, so make sure you don't shoot me by mistake!"

"Cousin, if I shoot you it won't be by mistake!" Jeff said grinning. Milton grinned back and led the way out the back door.

Jeff, rifle cocked, knelt down behind the corner and waited, thinking about his cousin. He admitted to himself what he would never have told his cousin: Milton was the better shot with a rifle, and when it came to being sneaky he could out-injun an injun. That Comanche would likely never know what had killed him.

The loud boom caught him by surprise. He leaned against the house and looked north toward the corral, expecting to see Milton. But there was no sign of him, and when he didn't show after a short time Jeff began to worry.

Could Milton have walked into an ambush? Had that Comanche allowed himself to be seen, hoping that an unsuspecting townsman would follow to where others waited?

Jeff had just decided to slip over to the corral when he spotted Milton loping toward him. Less than a minute later, they entered Jake's house, closing and barring the door behind them. Jeff glanced around, expecting to see the housekeeper, but there was no sign of her.

"I was getting a mite worried, Milt. What kept you?" he asked.

"I decided to reload while I had a chance, and since none of his friends had showed up by then I figured I might as well get something to remember him by. First man I ever killed, Jeff, and you know, collecting his scalp was easier than I figured! Just make a deep cut around that forelock and yank! Comes off slick as anything!" Milton held up the fresh scalp and grinned at his cousin, who shook his head and grinned back.

They stopped grinning when a fusillade of shots rang out.

"Guess there was more than one after all," Milton said. "We'll need the shotguns. I'll watch the front gate, you watch the back."

He turned toward the kitchen and squawked, "Hey, it's us!"

The housekeeper stopped, butcher knife in her right hand and a large cast-iron skillet raised to brain Milton in her left. "Laws! I wuz fair worried there for a minute!" she squawked.

"*You* were worried? You scared me out of a year's growth! But since you're here and this will likely not be over for a while, would you mind making a pot of coffee?"

***

The housekeeper brought two cups of coffee, but the cousins had no time to drink it.

Comanche warriors raced into Victoria, whooping and launching arrows and lances at terrified people running south along the road. Jeff's shotgun boomed, then boomed again before he laid it aside.

"Cover me, Milt! I'm going out to see if I can bring some of those poor people in here!"

Without waiting to see if Milton complied, Jeff unbolted the door and ran for the gate. Opening it, he waved frantically at two women carrying an infant and a toddler. Three other children ran close behind them, trying to keep up.

"In here! Jeff yelled, "and hurry! They're right behind you!"

Waiting only to see that they had heard him and were coming, Jeff stepped coolly into the street. Drawing his pistol, he cocked it and shot the leading warrior off his horse.

The Comanche barely had time to hit the ground before Jeff shot the one who'd been riding immediately behind his first victim.

He dodged between the terrified horses just as other Indians veered toward him. He cocked the pistol again and backed toward the gate, waiting for them to close the range.

Behind him, a shotgun boomed, the explosion followed almost immediately by another.

Kicking horses ran into others and by then, at least two Indians had fallen. Finally at the gate and ready to duck inside, Jeff lined up the revolver and shot at another, who immediately fell to the side. Jeff wondered for a moment if he'd killed the man, but the Comanche had leaned to his mount's off side so that only his lower leg and foot showed. He pulled back on his bowstring, preparing to launch a point-blank arrow at Jeff.

But then the horse hunched its back and grunted, a hoarse, guttural, dying exhalation. Jeff barely had time to duck away from spouting blood before the animal fell, trapping its rider.

He emptied the pistol into the crowd, then stepped through the gate and barred it behind him.

Turning, he ran for the door. The gate wouldn't hold them for long, and for that matter if they were determined enough, they might even hack their way through the house's front door or shutters.

He made up his mind to kill as many as possible before they did. Milton had known what to do; if you couldn't shoot the rider, shoot the horse. He checked the bar holding the shutters in place and peered through the small loophole, rifle ready.

"Can I help?" a soft voice asked. "I can shoot or reload, just as you please."

The young woman looked scared, but determined. Long brown hair, held in the back by a leather thong, and despite the scare she'd just had, quite self-possessed.

"Ever shot a rifle before?" Jeff asked. "Mine kicks some if you're not used to it."

"I've shot my father's Kentucky long-rifle, but if you're talking about the one like you're holding, then no. I've never shot one like that."

"Two things to remember, then. Hold on tight when you shoot, and the rear trigger sets the front one. Don't touch it until you're lined up on a target, then squeeze gently. Don't do more than needful, or you'll pull the shot off to the right."

"I can do that." She took the rifle from him and peered down the sights "Can you move to your right a bit so I can see better?"

Jeff moved aside and as she slid in to take his place by the loophole, he looked at her and wondered why he'd never noticed her before.

A girl that pretty? Why, a man would have to be blind not to pay attention to her!

Chapter Twenty-two

Jeff and Milton stayed put during the rest of the day, only shooting when a Comanche got close to the house.

After a time, they began avoiding the road out in front of the house in favor of breaking into houses up at the north end of town.

Penelope Rudd, for that was her name, had cleaned powder-fouled barrels and reloaded emptied weapons while Jeff and Milton kept watch, ready. During lulls, Jeff learned more about Penelope.

A falling tree limb had killed her father and a year later, her mother had died from smallpox. Neighbors had taken her in while they waited for a response from her uncle, who had agreed to take her in. But then had come the revolution.

She had seen little of her uncle John Linn while the war was going on, and along with many others, had fled east during the Runaway Scrape. He had eventually located her in Nacogdoches, where she'd taken refuge with a family who had recently lost a daughter to smallpox. He'd sent a letter to friends in Galveston, who had brought her south with them and paid her passage to Victoria.

She had only praise for John Linn; he'd kept her safe and when opportunity allowed, done what he could to educate her. But since her arrival, he had gone away often on business. And now had come the Comanche attack.

The woman who'd been with her when Jeff spotted them, and who now was helping the housekeeper in the kitchen, was a stranger. Penelope had seen her struggling and moved over to help her take care of the children.

Jeff and Milton took turns keeping watch, but as expected the Comanches rode away late that afternoon. They would fight during darkness only when there was no other option.

"No rifles tonight," said Jeff. "We wouldn't have light enough to aim, and if we do run into a Comanche it will be knife-fight close, so keep your pistol ready in your hand. First stop, the gun-shop, to pick up four revolvers. That way, we'll both have two and there'll be two for Penelope. Girl, you watch out for us coming back and don't be too quick to shoot!"

"I won't! You're getting pistols for me?"

"We are. Better you than a murdering Comanche, and I also reckon that you can handle them easier than a rifle. Bar the door as soon as we leave and don't open it back up unless it's one of us," Jeff said.

She nodded assent and after a quick look around outside, the cousins slipped away into the night.

The full moon, called by settlers a 'Comanche moon', cast shadows across the town. Toward the north end of Victoria, flames flickered red from a still-burning barn. The fitful light appeared to reveal movement when there was none, but both had seen the like before.

Milton led the way, while Jeff followed a short distance behind.

Entering the gun-shop by the back door, they located the pistols by feel. After gathering them up, they slipped back to the house.

The low flame of a candle their only light, they sat down a few feet away to load the cylinders. Not for the first time, they silently cursed the clumsy reloading process, made doubly-difficult by the poor lighting; but soon it was done.

Jeff called Penelope over and explained how the pistol functioned. "When you cock the hammer," he said, "the trigger will swing down. The hammer has a notch for sighting, but with the light the way it is you're better off if you just point and squeeze the trigger. Think you can do that?"

"I can," Penelope said quietly. "If there's time, I think I can reload it too."

"Good girl!" he said, and smiled. But she didn't smile back.

"That's the second time you've said that. For your information, I'm not a girl, Mister Bell!"

"I'm sorry, that just slipped out," Jeff said, flustered. From her expression, she was not mollified in the least.

But he would worry about that later; first, there was the matter of ensuring that the Indians had gone, and after that seeing whether their neighbors needed assistance.

Milton once again led as they slowly worked their way north, moving silently from house to house while listening for signs of life.

They found two families, and one hadn't been raided at all for reasons known only to the Comanches. The other family, by name Maverick, had sustained an injury.

An arrow had struck Sam's upper arm just before he reached the house. His wife Mary had broken the shaft just behind where the feathered end entered his arm, then pulled the arrow the rest of the way through. She had poured whiskey into the wound and bandaged it with a strip from a table-cloth.

He took a long swallow of the whiskey, then pulled a chair into position behind the shuttered window.

From then on, whenever he spotted an Indian he'd shot at him. He'd had no way to be sure, but thought he'd killed several.

To both families Jeff gave the same advice: "Everyone else is down at the south end, forted up. We've got room for you where we are, but if you have friends you might prefer to stay with them."

"Do you think they'll come back, Jeff?" asked Mary. She had just finished swapping Sam's bloody bandage for a fresh one.

"Ma'am, I just don't know. Jacob never expected them to raid us, but then I doubt he ever reckoned on there being at least a hundred of them, maybe more, in one war party!

"As to whether they'll be back, they stole whatever they could lay hands on up here in the north end of town but they never got past us. We killed some and wounded more, but since there's more plunder to be had and a few more scalps to collect, they might just decide to come back. They also might just figure it's time to go home with what they already got."

"What you're saying is that there's no telling," Mary said calmly, "so we need to act as if we were certain they would be back."

"Yes, ma'am. That's what I'm saying."

"How are you fixed for powder and shot?" Sam asked. "I fired off most of mine yesterday. I could have shot a few more of the devils, but I figured I had to keep some back. I reckon you know why."

"I understand," said Milton, "and yes, we've got both. But bring your bullet mold with you, in case your rifle is a different caliber.

"We've got lead enough to cast as many balls as you're likely to need, and as for powder, there's half of a keg of triple-F and another of double-F grade that hasn't been opened yet. We should be fine."

"You didn't mention Jake. He's not hurt, is he?" asked Mary.

"No, ma'am, not as far as I know. He went off with his partner Jean-Louis, trailing a herd of horses to Linnville for auction. Their families might be there already. They took the cutter, so they likely got there quicker."

"I hope they're all right," Mary said. "You don't think the Indians will go all the way down there, do you?"

"I hope not," Jeff said, "but none of us are safe now. I wonder if President Lamar knows what a hornet's nest he stirred up at the Council House?"

***

Time passed slowly after they returned.

"I doubt they'll be back, and probably not during the night, but as riled up as they are I don't reckon we can chance it. You want first watch or midnight to morning, Cousin?" asked Jeff.

"If they're coming back, they'll be here right after daybreak, so why don't I take the second watch?" suggested Milton.

"You get some sleep then, and at first rooster-crow, you wake me up. If they're not here by dawn, you and me will scout around and see how bad they tore things up."

"I don't think I can chance sleeping in a bed," Milton said. "I'll rustle up some bedding and make a pallet over against the wall. Wake me up if you hear anything." Jeff nodded, planning to take over the pallet after Milton got up.

"We'll fix breakfast after you get back, then," said Penelope.

"I would admire a cup of coffee now, if you don't mind," said Jeff.

Penelope smiled at him. "I'll be happy to! The beans are already roasted, so I'll just grind enough for a fresh pot! Be back in two shakes."

Jeff watched as she walked away. Was that a little extra wiggle? Maybe; she had to know he'd be watching! Was that what she meant by two shakes?

He felt like laughing, then decided he'd better not. She might ask what was so funny, and he'd never be able to explain!

He sipped the coffee and complimented her on the taste. She asked, "Mind if I sit up with you? I'm still nervous."

Jeff nodded, and she went on.

"Those poor people they caught! Some they scalped and just left the bodies a-laying in the road! But they made sure to pick up the ones *you* shot!"

"They do that," he said absently, peering through the loophole. "I hear it has to do with their beliefs. One that's killed is just reborn the same way he was, or maybe a little younger and not all achy and gray. But if he was scalped or his body mutilated, then that's the way he'll always be in the next life.

"The one that won't risk his life to pick up the body of another won't get picked up if *he* gets killed, so there's not much they won't do to carry their dead away."

"You know a lot about them!" exclaimed Penelope, smiling.

"Aw, people talk and I listen," Jeff blushed. He continued watching out the window.

She remained nearby and continued to talk until it was time for him to wake Milton.

She sure was easy to talk to, he thought. *Pretty, too. And no slouch in the kitchen!*

***

Milton shook him awake before dawn. "Nothing stirring. Still of a mind to look around?"

"I reckon. Any of that coffee left?"

"Maybe, but you'd better wait. I've heard old-timers claim that Indians can smell coffee on your breath, or whatever it was that you last had to eat. If you're too sleepy, I'll go out alone."

"Not *that* sleepy, Cousin! Just let me get my powder horn and possibles bag and I'll be ready."

As before, they moved cautiously. Milton led, while Jeff watched, rifle ready. As soon as Milton had found concealment where he could watch ahead, Jeff moved up to join him. After a brief pause, they repeated.

Dead horses lay in the dusty street, and near them, dark splotches showed where Comanches had fallen. But they saw no evidence that any of Victoria's residents were still hiding in the north end of the town.

Nor were there any signs that the Indians had come back.

A few houses had been burned or had their doors chopped open, but the damage was less than they'd feared.

"I reckon we can rebuild," observed Jeff softly.

"I never doubted it. You hungry?"

"I could eat," agreed Jeff. "Lead the way, I'll follow."

***

Penelope was as good as her word when they got back. "Eggs, potatoes, smoked side-meat, and a fresh pot of coffee! Dig in!"

"I didn't notice any eggs when looked in the kitchen yesterday," Jeff said.

"I figured it was safe. If there were Indians around, you would have been shooting, so I went out to the chicken coop and collected as many as I could find. Good thing the Indians didn't get the hens!"

They were sitting at the table, finishing their second cups of coffee when they heard the first shot. It was followed by a rapid drumming of hooves and the screeching whoops of warriors.

"Penelope, make sure that back door is barred! And get your pistols! Cousin, sounds like they're close enough for the shotguns. Buck and ball, right?"

"Yeah, and with our rifles handy for when they pull back," said Milton. Moments later, his shotgun boomed, then bare seconds later boomed again. "Fetched a couple," he said, his satisfaction obvious, "and I reckon the buckshot hit a horse or two. Sure is a passel of 'em!"

Jeff's rifle cracked, and out in the street a screech broke off in mid-whoop. "Missed! I was aiming at his horse, but he leaned over just as I shot! But it doesn't seem like there are as many as there were yesterday."

Milton nodded and went on with the task of reloading the shotgun.

"Don't fret, Jeff. You'll get one of their horses the next time," said Penelope. "I can't help but feel sorry for the poor animals. They didn't choose to come here!"

"I don't like shooting horses either, but some say they value horses more than they do their wives. I don't reckon it matters, but if they have to walk to their next fight, then maybe they'll stay at home!"

***

Around midday, with last defiant whoops, the Comanches thundered out of Victoria.

But no one thought of going outside. They waited, still alert to the possibility that it was a trick. It was an old tactic for the Indians, pretending they had gone in order to draw pursuers into a trap.

The sun was just going down when the first riders slipped into Victoria. "They're Texians, Milton!" Penelope exclaimed. "Look, there are more of them!"

The riders were the first visible evidence, but dismounted rangers and militiamen had already infiltrated between the houses, looking for any evidence that an Indian had remained behind.

But they'd gone, and with them they'd taken their wounded and dead. By ones and twos, the men who'd defended Victoria walked out to join the newcomers.

Jeff cracked the shutter and called out, "Don't shoot! There are women and children in here!" In response, several riders split away and headed for the house.

"Mind if we come in, Sir?" their leader asked.

"Light and set, and welcome!" called Penelope. "I'm right

glad to see you! We all are!"

Suspicious, his hand hovering over the butt of his holstered revolver, the man walked inside and looked around to make sure that no Indian was present.

Satisfied, he relaxed and walking to the door, called out to the waiting men. "These folks are okay. How about the rest?"

"Some wounded down toward the south end of town, Captain. Ain't seen no more dead ones, but I reckon we'll get a count directly and we can add that rancher and his slave to the ones killed here."

"They overran a ranch?" asked Milton.

"No, the Comanches surprised them while they were working in one of the fields."

"You said that one was a slave?" asked Jeff.

The captain nodded, puzzled. "I did. Black or white, who you are don't make no never-mind to them unless you're a Comanche; everybody else is an enemy. Why do you ask?"

"We're apprenticed to Jacob Jennings, the gunsmith," Jeff explained. "He's got a rancho north of town and his partner Jean-Louis has a horse ranch up that way too. We've been worried, because we've got friends among the crews.

"But neither one will own slaves, so I'm guessing the two men you mentioned came from another spread."

"Likely," agreed the captain. "But they raided that horse ranch you mentioned. Stole a few head, best we could figure, but never managed to break into the house so the people are all safe. We spoke to them on our way here and they fixed us a meal, which was mighty nice of them."

"So what happened to the Comanches?" asked Milton. "There were hundreds of them! Biggest war party I've ever heard of!"

"You're right about that," the captain confirmed. "We can only guess at their numbers, but the scouts figure there must have been at least a thousand of them!"

"A thousand warriors?" asked Penelope. "You're sure? I didn't know there were that many in all of Texas!"

"No, Miss. Likely half are warriors, maybe a mite more than

that, but they'll have brought women along to do camp work and such. Children, too. But don't be fooled by that, because they're not like us. Their women and even their children fight.

"As for which way they went after they left here, we found where they camped yesterday over on Spring Creek. But they didn't go back there after they left this morning. We followed their trail, and they were heading south."

"Toward Linnville?"

"Afraid so, Miss. Ain't nothing else down that way big enough to interest that many Indians!"

Chapter Twenty-three

We left the men to look after the herd and Jean-Louis and me headed to town. On the way we passed John Linn's wharf.

"I see that folks are already shipping cotton," Jean-Louis observed.

"Weather's been good, but a body never knows how long it will last down here. I 'spect they picked what they could before the fall rains start."

"Likely you're right," Jean-Louis agreed. "There's the cutter, so the womenfolks made it to town all right. They'll either be at the hotel or out on the street investigating the stores!"

I was glad to see Priscilla and Little Ed, and Jean-Louis made a fuss over Sharon and baby Angie. Both wives were spruced up for walking out in town, but they'd have to wait on me. I needed a bath and a change of clothes before I'd be fit to be seen with them, and even Jean-Louis looked like he needed a good clean-up! So we promised to meet them back at the hotel after we were done.

I got a trim and a barber shave, then had my bath. Jean-Louis had bathed first, and he sat down in the chair after I got up to get his haircut and shave.

By the time I got to our hotel room, Priscilla had my new store-bought suit and dress boots laid out ready.

I barely had time to open my mouth before she started in. "Don't think you're the only one!" she said. "Sharon is having a talk with Jean-Louis right now! You are important men and it's time the Republic recognized it, but it won't happen if you walk around a town as big as Linnville in torn and dirty Levi's pants! And that's not all, that hat of yours will *never* do! As soon as you're dressed, we'll stop in at Robinson's store and get you one that's suitable for a rancher and businessman!"

"This is about you and Sharon, isn't it?" I said. "You don't want to be seen with a couple of men who work for a living, do you?" Right away I wished I could pull them words back, but I couldn't and I knowed I was in deep trouble. She turned red as a Texas sunset, which told me I had hit the mark dead center, and as every married man knows that ain't a good sign. She wasn't going to let up, Sharon neither. There would be no peace until they got us dressed up to look like a pair of whiskey drummers, or worse, politicians! Ain't a working man yet that didn't go right out and buy himself a store-bought suit as soon as somebody called him 'Judge' or 'Senator'! But I figured to have one more try, just to show her I wasn't tamed.

"John Linn is a lot more important than *we* are, and *he* doesn't wear a fancy hat!"

When she grinned at me I knowed I'd lost. "He's got one now, a tall silk hat that came all the way from New York!" So I shut up and got into that suit.

It fit tolerably well, though it was nowhere near as comfortable as my old work clothes. At least she'd knowed better than to try talking me into town shoes! I played with Little Ed for a few minutes and soon had him laughing fit to bust, but when Priscilla started tapping her foot I handed him over to the nanny.

She nearly exploded again when I strapped my pistol on.

"You can't wear that! Your coat won't hang right! And besides, you'll need a new cane to complete your outfit! All the city men have them, and you're a business man as well as a gunsmith! It's time for you to *look* like a businessman, and that means a nice cane! If you were wearing that pistol, you would look funny with your cane banging into that pistol grip with every step!"

"I'll switch the holster to my left side," I said, "but I'm going to wear my pistol. I *want* people to see it, so that some of the town men you're so hot to have me look like will want one themselves!

Sam Colt has starting shipping his new-model pistols to Texas, so I need to sell the ones I've got while I can."

Well, I won *that* scrap, but I knowed things were likely to be chillier than a Texas norther for a while.

We stopped in at Robinson's and she picked out a silk

stovepipe hat, but I passed on her idea of a cane. Fancy, it was, black, and with silver inlays, but instead, I got a plain black one with a sword inside.

I remembered that not all that many years ago, a man had stuck a cane-sword in Jim Bowie's chest during that sandbar fight, before Jim got mad and gutted him with that big fighting knife of his.

Town men don't carry Bowie knives, but I would have bet good silver money that half the canes they carried were like mine, a wooden sheath hiding the blade inside.

Nearly as soon as we walked out of the store I spotted John Linn, and he saw me at about the same time. "Jacob! I've got some folks here you need to meet!"

So we walked over and tipped my new hat to the young woman, then nodded at the man. "Jacob Jennings, meet Hugh Watts and his new bride Juliet Constance! They've only been married about three weeks!"

"Congratulations, Mister Watts! I wish you and your lady every happiness!" Inside, I was plumb happy with myself. Not even Jean-Louis could have said it better!

John noticed too, but didn't say anything, because just then, Jean-Louis and Sharon walked up so the introductions started over again.

Until I interrupted them, and to this day I don't know quite how it happened.

One minute I was standing there like a clothes dummy, the next I'd somehow managed to draw my pistol, swap hands, and shoot a Comanche warrior who'd been about to throw his spear at one of us.

Jean-Louis looked surprised, the women couldn't figure out what had happened, and John Linn was frowning up a storm after I did it. But as soon as I pointed at that Comanche, laying on the ground with the bullet hole in his face that was still oozing blood, they all figured out what had happened. The yells and screeching war-whoops that broke out before the gunshot had stopped echoing let us know the one I'd shot hadn't come alone.

Jean-Louis had been wearing his revolver too, and by now he had it in his hand, cocked and ready.

"Jake?" he asked.

"Waterfront; they won't have come from that direction. Mister Linn?"

"I agree," John said calmly. He was holding a twister-pistol, one with two barrels that city men often carried, and he looked like he was ready to use it. "Hugh, are you armed?"

"No, John. But they're not here yet, so you go on ahead; I need to pick up my watch before some savage runs off with it. Juliet, you go with them, and after I get my watch I'll catch up."

"Not without you! I'll wait here, so hurry!" she exclaimed.

"John, we can't wait for him," I said softly. "Judging by the noise, they're almost here, and we've got families to think of!"

"You're right, Jacob. Ladies, if you'll oblige us by heading for my wharf, we'll follow. Gentlemen, I think that line abreast behind the ladies would suit us well?"

That's what we did, me with the sword in my left hand, my revolver in my right. The wooden cane part had fallen off somewhere.

I figured I could do without it, but that bare blade might come in handy.

Looking back to where we'd come from, I saw no sign of Hugh Watts or his new wife. But he'd made his choice, and a man has to live with it. I felt sorry for his wife, but I had my own to look after.

It seemed like we was never going to get to that wharf, but time is funny that way. When you really need to hurry, seems like you're always short of time, but when you're enjoying something it never lasts as long as a body would prefer.

John looked behind us and said, "That's disappointing. I had hoped my men hadn't loaded the cotton bales."

"You figured to fort up back of them, with the bay behind so that they couldn't surround us?" I asked.

"Just so," he agreed, still calm. "Gentlemen, I fear we have few options at this point. They are too many for three men to fight off. 'Tis not what I would have chosen, but better companions I couldn't ask for."

"We're not done for yet," I said. "John, they're plains Indians and they don't savvy water at all. I suggest we put the women and babies in that boat," I pointed at one drawn up on the sand, "and row them out to my ship."

Jean-Louis nodded. "John, that's our *Eureka* just beyond the schooner. Why don't you row the ladies out there while Jake and I gather up as many people as we can? We'll join you directly, even if we have to wade."

John nodded and after he was ready, oars out, my family behind him and Jean-Louis's in front, we shoved the boat off and John commenced rowing.

We turned back and when we spotted people, waved as hard as we could for them to join us. As soon as they saw us, they headed our way, with more behind them, all following the ones that looked like they knowed where to go.

Seemed like they were never going to stop coming!

But both ships had noticed what we were doing and sent their boats to help. They stopped just off the beach long enough for us to hurry the ladies into the shallow water, pushing when we had to. They didn't look none too happy with us, but they got in the boats and none of them got shot or captured, so I reckon we done good.

While this was going on, a Comanche would get too brave now and again and one of us would take a shot at him. Whether we hit him or not didn't much matter; they didn't know there were only two of us with a pistol apiece, so they stayed out of range.

Mine was empty and Jean-Louis's empty or nearly so when the people stopped coming.

We decided we'd done all we could and boarded Eureka's boat. That nervous coxswain had his crew bending their oars so that we fairly flew across the water! In hardly any time, we were climbing on deck and there was Captain Matthews to welcome us.

With a gaggle of women, kids, and a few men from the town standing around on deck behind him gawking at us.

We shook hands and then I took charge. "Captain, get the women and children belowdecks if there's room, in the cabins if there's not. Have you loaded the cannons?"

"Not yet, Sir. We've been busy…" he started.

The Comanches were attacking and he hadn't even thought to load the guns! "Send me two reliable hands," I interrupted. "Open the magazine and issue weapons, such of them as you have. Jean-Louis, you would oblige me if you would take command of the larboard guns?"

"Aye, aye…" he said, then broke off. I grinned at him and he grinned back. We both knowed he'd been about to call me 'Sir', but as we were partners it wouldn't do.

Matthews went on his way and soon the two men I'd asked for came up. One was carrying a small powder barrel, the other a bag of musket balls in each hand.

"Let me guess," I said. "No cartridge bags?"

"No, Sir," the man said stolidly. Not for him the responsibility; that was for the master and the mate.

"Very well. Do we at least have a powder ladle?" I asked.

"Yes, Sir. I'll be getting it directly, Sir, by your leave."

"Two, if you have that many aboard," I said. "Otherwise, I suppose Jean-Louis and I will have to share." He nodded and hurried away. He detoured to larboard on his way back to hand Jean-Louis one of the ladles.

Even so, it took longer than it should have to load. But we got it done, and then we waited.

In the town, the Comanches had it all to themselves. Like so many human cockroaches, they ran into and out of houses, but soon gave that up in favor of the stores. And every time they came out of one, they brought an armload of plunder.

I figured they would never have a use for some of it, but they didn't care. Whatever took their fancy, they stole.

Umbrellas. Suits of clothes. Dresses, everything they could carry, they brought out.

They hated whites and Mexicans alike, but now that they had the chance, they copied us as best they could.

The longer I watched, the madder I got, and I wasn't the only one. Judge John Hays was fairly jumping up and down when he wasn't pacing the deck and shaking his fist at the Indians.

"Captain Matthews," I said, "if you please, I'd admire if you would have a spring line rigged to both anchor lines. I intend to shift our position enough to use the starboard guns first, then swing about so the port guns will bear. Keep the crew at their work, because as soon as I fire they'll be needed."

"Yes, Sir. Ah, Sir…are you sure you want to fire into the town?" Matthews asked.

"There's not much reason not to, in my judgement," I said. "Just look at them!" On shore, whooping Comanches raced their horses down Linnville's main road and as soon as they'd reached the far end, they spun their mounts and raced back. Some wore looted coats and more than one was wearing the garment backwards, with the buttons behind him.

Others had top hats that they were holding in place with one hand while controlling their mounts with the other. Some waved umbrellas, most turned inside-out by the wind from their racing horses. A horse raced the length of the street, with the rider holding onto the end of a bolt of blue cloth that was unrolling behind.

"You'll not be firing your great guns into Linnville, Jacob."

John Linn had walked up while I was busy getting ready. "Our stores have been emptied, our warehouses too, but when this is finished we'll restock and go on. But if you destroy the buildings, I don't know what might happen."

"What if the *Comanches* destroy your buildings, John?" I asked softly.

"They may, Jacob, they may. But they may not, and I will not see my town destroyed to save it."

"And if they find boats?" I asked.

"Then I'll pay you a bounty for every boat you sink, and damn the buildings!"

***

The day passed slowly.

Eureka's crew and our passengers watched silently as the Comanches continued their work of destruction. From what I could see, people on the schooner were doing the same. Most were too shocked to do anything else.

With one exception. I hadn't noticed at the time, but Judge Hays had picked up a shotgun and let himself down into the rowboat that John had used to bring our families to safety. I didn't notice the gun until after he got close enough to shore to jump out of the boat, but then I saw him waving it overhead as he waded on to the sand, shrieking as loud as any Comanche!

"That damned fool! He's going to get himself killed!" said John Linn.

"Or captured. I wonder if he had time to load that shotgun?" I asked.

He hadn't. I saw him pointing it at the Comanches and repeatedly trying to fire it.

Surprisingly, after their first astonishment, several had come to the water's edge and now they stood there staring at him. Finally, exhausted, he simply sat down in the shallow water and waited for what might happen, fury spent.

"They think he's crazy," John said wonderingly. "They figure it's bad medicine to harm a crazy person!"

"*I* may, when he gets back! I'll bet the seawater has ruined that shotgun!"

***

Late that afternoon, tired from all the riding or simply bored by the whole thing, the Indians began to leave. By ones and twos, clutching whatever had caught their fancy on their horses or leading a packed mule or horse, they slowly rode away.

Among the last were the captives, most already showing evidence of abuse.

"Jacob, did you mark who that third woman was?" asked John Linn softly.

"Yes, Sir. She's been beaten, looks like, and she's bruised up some. But judging by the hair and her dress, that's Juliet Watts."

"The widow Watts, now, I shouldn't wonder," said John. "I hope so. If they took him alive, he'll be a long time dying."

There was nothing to say.

The man had been a fool to value a watch above his wife, but he had either paid for his folly or soon would.

Behind them, pillars of smoke thickened and the first flames shot up.

The Comanches, in one last fit of rage, had torched Linnville.

Chapter Twenty-four

"I'm just glad you fellers got here when you did, but I'm a mite surprised too," Jeff said.

"We were warned," said Adam Zumwalt, captain of the Lavaca militia. "I reckon the men who came to tell us that the Comanches were out in force figured the fight was over after that first day. First time I ever heard of them sticking around after a raid!

"Ben McCulloch is on the way here too; he sent a rider from Gonzales to let me know, and John Tumlinson is assembling a company of volunteers right here in Victoria."

"We'll talk to him," Milton said. "Where will he get horses? I doubt there's a single live horse in Victoria, and judging by what you said earlier, there aren't any in the vicinity."

"We're bringing extras, probably enough for all of you," Zumwalt said. "I'll bet John will be glad to have you two along! I hear you put up a good fight!"

"We killed a few," Jeff said, and Milton nodded assent.

"More than a few, the way others tell it," Zumwalt observed. "But I need to get back to my men, so I'll talk to you later. Ma'am?" he nodded farewell to Penelope, who nodded back.

"Milton, we need to mold a bunch of balls before we take off," Jeff said. "Penelope, if you would oblige me by stoking the fireplace while we bring the molds and a pound or two of lead?"

She did, and while the molds were warming at the edge of the fire and the lead in the ladle was melting, the cousins refilled their powder horns. After a search through the gun-shop, they also found powder flasks with spouts designed to deliver a precise amount of powder to the pistol chambers. They topped the flasks off with powder and added them to their possibles bags. While they were busy preparing, Penelope and the other women cooked a meal and wrapped packs of jerky for them to take along.

They ate rapidly, Jeff thanked the women and cautioned them to be careful, then the two headed off to look for Captain Tumlinson.

"You ever meet him, Cousin?" Jeff asked.

"Not that I recall," admitted Milton. "Probably lots of folks in Victoria that we don't know because they don't come in to the gun-shop and we don't go visiting in the town. I reckon you'd have remembered Penelope!"

Jeff blushed, but said nothing. He definitely would *not* have forgotten her! For a moment, he wondered; what would she say after this was all over if he asked her to go walking out? Or would it be more proper to ask her guardian first?

He was still mulling over the question when they found John Tumlinson, who immediately put them to work.

"Jeff, you're company first sergeant and Milton, you're second sergeant. Your job is to make sure the men have balls and powder enough for an extended campaign, and Jeff, I want you to inspect their weapons. I had to send one man away because all he had was an old flintlock musket!"

"We've got rifles for them that need one, but we'll be wanting them back after the fighting," Jeff said.

John said he'd see to it and the cousins went off to carry out their duties. "I figured to enlist as a private," said Jeff. "First sergeant? I don't know anything about being a sergeant!"

"Neither do I," said Milton. "Makes a man wonder about the quality of the volunteers! But at least we understand the jobs he gave us."

"Yep," agreed Jeff. "And because he knowed what needed to be done, I figure he knows how to be a captain."

By midmorning, mounted on borrowed horses and with several of the men armed with borrowed rifles, the volunteers, now part of a joint force with the Lavaca militia, rode out of Victoria.

Burdened by the plunder from Victoria and Linnville, and by the three thousand horses they had captured, the Comanches could move no faster than a slow walk.

The gaggle of militia companies and volunteers caught up

with them that afternoon.

***

"We've got them, boys!" said Captain Zumwalt. "They'll not willingly surrender a single horse, nor jot or tittle of what they stole!"

"You'll not charge that many Comanches, will you," asked Tumlinson anxiously.

"I'll not be so foolhardy!" Zumwalt responded. "I propose to close with them until their drag riders are in range of our rifles and shoot them down. With no one to push from behind, the horses will slow even more. If the Comanches fire back, so much the better! The animals will scatter to the point that the savages will be unable to recover them, but *we* shall do so as soon as we've taught them to never again raid a Texas town!"

"That's Mercado Creek up ahead," Jeff pointed out. "And beyond that's Casa Blanca creek. Both have fairly high banks in this area, so a few riflemen might be able to delay them long enough for the other companies you mentioned to come up with us."

"Capital idea, Sir, a capital idea! Captain Tumlinson, I would be much obliged if you would take your command to the west. I will attack from the east, and as soon as you hear my men open fire, do you join in!"

***

Once we were sure that the Indians had gone, we managed to round up a few of Jean-Louis's horses. The raiders had gotten most of them, but some had escaped into the swampy areas along Garcitas Cove and we were able to trap them by herding them toward the water. After several men were mounted, the work became easier.

I spotted Ed Burleson among the dusty riders who rode into the ruined town that afternoon. He saw us too and waved, so me and Jean-Louis rode over to tell him what had happened.

After I finished, I asked what his plans were and offered to join him.

"Of course, and I'm happy to have your assistance. By the

181

way, I thank you for the gift you sent me, but I now have a replacement. This is one of Sam Colt's new 'Texas' models, the same as our new Ranger company has."

"Ranger Company?" I asked. I was familiar with ranging companies, but this sounded different.

"Jack Hays is their captain," Ed explained, "and a fine one he is, despite his appearance! He's of middling height only, and well-mannered almost to a fault until he smells powder smoke, but then he earns the nickname his men have given him. Devil Jack, indeed!

"Speaking of captains, I have volunteers who've not been assigned to a company. I'll take you around and introduce you and if they'll have you as their captain, will you serve?"

I just nodded. Seemed like Ed was forever appointing me to one thing or another, and I wanted to rejoin my family, but I figured that would have to wait. John Linn would see that they were kept safe.

Jean-Louis only nodded, so I guessed he felt like I did.

A rider rode up right after he introduced me to my new company. "Colonel, the Comanches are heading north. Far as we can tell, they circled around east of the upriver settlements and turned south to get here, and that's the same way they're going back. Smart of them, otherwise we would have gotten a warning that they were on the warpath."

"They're savages, but they're not stupid and they're certainly no stranger to warfare!" Ed observed. "They fought other Indians before the Europeans arrived, and after that the Spanish and Mexicans. They're bound to have learned everything there is to know about staying out of sight. What else do you have for me?"

"They forded the San Marcos up by where Plum Creek flows in," the scout said, "and then crossed the Guadalupe just below the big bend. From there, they went southeast until after they'd passed Gonzales, then turned due south for Victoria."

"I had hoped that we could cut cross-country," Ed said, "but from your description that won't be possible."

He paused for a moment, thinking about what the scout had reported.

"Well, then," he said briskly, "we'll simply have to follow as fast as we can. Captain Jennings, mount your company and join us as soon as convenient."

I nodded, knowing that convenience had nothing to do with it.

"Jean-Louis, you're my lieutenant," I said. He nodded, expecting it.

"Volunteers!" I bellowed. "Mount up! You'll talk among yourselves as we ride and choose first and second sergeants from among you! I'll meet with them during our next stop!"

***

Tumlinson's volunteers handed their horses over to four older men, who would hold them while the others crept closer to the Comanches who were trailing the herd of stolen horses toward Mercado Creek.

Buckskin-clad scouts led those with less experience, most of whom were town residents. Jeff went with one that the men called Goat, while Milton was assigned, along with Captain Tumlinson, to a Tejano called Fernando. A hundred yards behind them came the rest of the company.

Jeff slipped into position behind a large pin-oak tree and squirmed into a comfortable seated position. The pistol was in the way, so he moved it around until he felt comfortable. Then he waited.

For the moment, none of the Comanches were in view, but he could hear their shrill yips as they chivvied reluctant horses toward the low bluffs lining the creek. He pointed his rifle between the trees and tried to relax as he waited for a target to appear.

Yips changed to alarmed whoops as soon as the first rifles fired, the explosions muffled by the trees. Tensely, Jeff waited, watching the narrow opening where he expected to sight a passing Indian.

A dozen horses raced past, then the first Comanche appeared.

But he was there and gone before Jeff could aim. Swearing to himself, he shifted his aim farther left, to where the Comanche had been hidden by the trees, and pulled the rear trigger, setting the front one so that the slightest squeeze would fire the rifle.

And waited, watching the right side of the opening. He would get no more than a split-second's warning…and there the man was, the tails of his feathered warbonnet trailing behind his galloping horse. Without thinking, Jeff touched the hair-trigger and the rifle bucked against his shoulder.

As the smoke cleared, he thought at first that he'd missed. But as he reloaded, he heard a faint cough from behind the clump of trees, followed by the rustling of dead leaves.

Off to his left came more shots and shrill whoops, accompanied by the drumming of hooves. But there was nothing to see.

Finally, rifle reloaded, he eased to his feet.

There was still nothing in view, and the shooting from his left was now farther away. Prowling forward, senses alert for anything, he slipped from tree to tree, pausing behind each bit of cover.

The Indian he'd shot had managed to sit up and was now leaning against a tree. His bow lay by his hand, but no arrow was visible and the man had heard Jeff's almost-silent approach.

For a moment, Jeff wondered whether he should approach closer, then saw the knife that was nearly concealed in the warrior's hand.

Shifting the rifle to his left hand, he drew his revolver, aimed, and shot the man through the forehead. As the smoke cleared, he aimed again, but held his fire. The Comanche still leaned back against the tree, but he was clearly dead. Even so, Jeff decided to take no chances. He paused long enough to reload the fired, then circled to his right and slipped up behind the leaning man.

Milton had been right. One circling cut with his knife, a single hard yank, and the scalp peeled off easily.

This one might make it to their hunting grounds, Jeff thought, *but he won't be happy when he gets there!*

Chapter Twenty-five

Ed Burleson drove us hard, wanting to get there before the fight started.

"I'll tell you, Jake," he said, "whoever is in charge will need a curb bit to rein in Jack Hays and his bunch of fire-eaters!"

"He's the Ranger captain?" I asked, wanting to be sure.

"He is, and a warrior from who flung the chunk! I don't reckon you've heard much about him, but he's related to Andy Jackson and a personal friend of Sam Houston. Got an Apache named Flacco that rides with him and leads the charge, which naturally makes that bunch of kids try harder!"

"An *Apache*? If he's a chief, wouldn't he be back with his tribe?"

"A body would think so," Ed agreed. "Maybe he used to be a chief. The title don't mean all that much, 'cause tribes swap chiefs whenever they figure the current one has lost his medicine. But Flacco's not the only Indian riding with Jack Hays. Placido is a Tonkawa and a real chief, because he's head of Jack's scouts. Thirteen of them there are, and they figure the sun comes up because Jack gives his okay every morning. But the main reason they're there is because they purely hate the Comanches."

"Hays sounds like my kind of Texan," I ventured. "After what I saw in Linnville, I reckon it's time we made the Comanches understand that Texans ain't Mexicans. Not that I'm blaming them for what they did, them not having as many people or as many soldiers back then as we do now.

"But we've got families to protect and if doing that means clearing every last Comanche out of Texas, then I reckon it's time we got to it."

"It's likely that you'll get your chance, Jake. How are your men shaping up?"

"About like you'd figure, Ed. They're here, and they'll do

their duty. I wouldn't call 'em fire-eaters, because they're not eager, but they've got a determination about 'em that makes me figure they'll keep on fighting as long as they've got a bullet left. And after that they'll go at 'em with knives."

"They're a mite older than the rangers," Ed observed, "but that means they're steadier, and they'll think before goin' sky-hootin' off after every Indian they see.

"One of these days, those rangers are going to bite off more than they can chew but I wouldn't expect that of your volunteers.

"I know most of those men personally, Jake. They'll do. And speakin' of them, you'd better be getting back because we'll be moving out directly."

After I got back, I met with Jean-Louis and the first sergeant the men had elected to pass on what Ed had told me.

"Gus? I didn't expect to see *you* here, but I'm glad you made it. I was a mite worried."

"They come sniffin' around," Gus grinned, "but I sicced m' dogs on 'em! It's one thing for them to scare off one of *their* dogs, but my bear dogs didn't pay 'em no mind! They went right for the hind legs on their horses, figuring to cripple 'em like they would a bear, and them Comanches skedaddled!"

I chuckled. "Ed says we'll be moving out directly, so I'll depend on you to keep our men closed up."

"I got a question for you, Captain. You like eating the dust of that Bastrop bunch?" Gus asked.

"Not particularly. Why do you ask?"

"I can have the men mount up right now and move out without waiting on Ed. Ain't like we don't know where we're going; the Comanches left a trail a blind man could follow!"

I looked at Jean-Louis and he grinned at me, so I nodded to Gus. "Mount the troop, First Sergeant."

Ed's Bastrop boys frowned a lot when we rode past, but I saw Ed trying to keep from grinning. He put his hand down where his men wouldn't see and gave me a little wave, so I knowed he wasn't mad at me for jumping the gun.

***

We were all tired by the time the shadows got long, but when that Indian stepped out from behind a tree, I heard the click behind me of rifles being cocked. I put my arms up and waved them to the side, wanting the men to move up in line abreast so they wouldn't shoot me by mistake.

That was when that Indian started yelling. "Me Tonkaway! Me Tonkaway!" And before you could say scat, he was back behind his tree.

"Jean-Louis, send two men ahead to check," I said. "The rest of us will deploy into line and be ready if they run into trouble."

I felt kind of proud that I remembered that. Hang around the army long enough and most anybody learns how to talk their language!

Jean-Louis nodded at one of the men near the front and the two of them took off for where that Indian had been.

I was only a little surprised, and it didn't last long. I should have figured that Jean-Louis would want to be out in front! I never had figured out which Lafitte he was related to, but from what I'd heard none of them was backward when it came to fighting!

The Indian was indeed a Tonkawa, and a scout for Jack Hays' Rangers. He led us to where they were resting and we dismounted, ready for a break ourselves. Hays offered me a cup of coffee that I was glad to get, and after I introduced Jean-Louis and Gus one of the rangers brought them coffee too. "I'll need the cups back when you're finished, Captain," he said. "They belong to the men."

I nodded and asked him to thank the owners.

We had time to finish our coffee and they didn't exactly hurry us, but the fires were being put out before we were done and we knew what that meant. Five minutes later, we were mounted.

Hays' troop didn't need to be told what to do. They gigged their mounts into an extended lope, so we did too and were back to eating dust.

The horses had doubtless expected more of a rest, but nobody had asked them and spurs were a powerful argument when one tried to balk.

***

Two hours later, I heard a boom from up ahead.

187

Jack Hays wasted no time. "At them, men!" He yelled something after that about teaching them to respect Texians, but I doubt anyone heard it, including him. Racing hooves drowned him out and suddenly he realized that if he intended to lead his men into battle, he'd better get cracking!

Which reminded me that *we'd* come to fight, not just ride across the country. I looked around and saw only determined faces, so I waved my revolver over my head and gigged my horse.

Good thing I did, otherwise they would have run right over me!

I thought to check my horse when I saw the body of a white woman, but she was beyond help. A bloody patch above her slack forehead showed that they'd taken the time after killing her to collect her scalp.

I had been a tad nervous up to that time. Now, that went away and I felt a killing rage rise up to take its place.

I vowed right then I'd collect a few Comanche scalps myself.

Part of me knowed that being dead, he wouldn't feel it. But if it sent a message to the rest, letting them know that for Texians it was war to the knife, they just might know a little of how I felt.

I 'spect I wasn't the only one, and when we spotted that dead child, scalped, and with an arrow buried to the feathers in his crumpled little body, it only made the men madder. But we were worried too, because it meant that the Comanches knowed we were closing in on them. And they had begun killing their captives, rather than chance us rescuing them.

Right after that, I started seeing horses standing or trotting away and it gave me an idea. "Jean-Louis! Help me stop the men!" I yelled.

I had to do it again before he understood, and he gave me a look of utter astonishment. "Our horses are nearly blown," I explained, "but the ones we're seeing are fresh! Get Gus to help you and start the men to switching mounts!"

He understood then, and within fifteen minutes the men were remounted and back in the chase. All we had to do was follow the dust and listen for where the shooting was.

That's when I spotted a familiar face leaning back against a tree. It was Juliet Watts, and she had an arrow sticking out of her chest but she was alive. I pointed to one of the men and waved to her, so he pulled up and went over to help.

The fresh horses helped. Didn't take long before we were even with Ed's boys and when they saw us fogging past, I reckon they figured out what we'd done.

We were soon mixed in with Hays' rangers, who hadn't swapped mounts. Jean-Louis and me were armed like they were, with pistols, but they had the newer version that Colt had started selling. They could reload by swapping out empty cylinders for loaded ones, which we couldn't; but since the fight had turned into a running battle, with men stopping to give their horses a breather from time to time, we kept up tolerably well.

We came up to Plum Creek and by then, we'd lost most of our men. It was just Jack Hays, Ed Burleson, Jean-Louis and me in the lead, with maybe half a dozen men behind us who'd caught up slower mounts when we swapped.

"They've split up," Ed said. "No telling which way they went."

"What of our men," I asked. "How many did we lose in the fighting?"

"None that I saw," said Jack. "But I'm plumb disappointed in my boys, and I intend they know my feelings when I catch them! They're *looting*! They broke off the fight to collect whatever the Comanches stole! *Bastards*!"

Ed looked plumb shocked at this. He'd told me that Jack Hays was mannerly, but this sure didn't sound that way! I understood his feelings. I hadn't seen any of ours fall either, but they weren't behind us, not even Gus.

"Let's head back and start rounding them up," Ed said. "We had the Comanches on the run, but if they manage to regroup and come at us we could still lose this fight!"

So we headed back. Along the way I spotted Juliet Watts and the man I'd sent to help her. He had the arrow out and she was bleeding, but from the look on her face she would live through this. I pulled up and nodded at her, but my question was for the volunteer who'd been helping.

"Ain't as bad as it looks, Captain. One of the young bucks shot her, but the arrow just barely poked through her corset!"

"They couldn't figure how to get it off me," Juliet said, "but he tried to shoot me anyway. I think he would have killed me but your men were so close that he didn't have time to make sure. I thank you for sending this gentlemen to assist me!"

***

I had lost track of Jean-Louis and Gus while I talked to Missus Watts, but I finally caught up to him by a campfire. I went over and he introduced me to General Felix Huston, who'd come up in time to take command.

I said howdy, but he was clearly busy so we went off to find our men.

"Jake, our boys didn't do anything that the others didn't. We're all volunteers, so I wouldn't say anything to them about looting. They might just decide to go home with what they got and we're going to need them tomorrow. General Huston told me that his spies have located the Indian camp up ahead of us and one spotted Buffalo Hump. He was talking to a bunch of warriors, at least a hundred, and more were coming in."

I figured it was good advice, and after telling Gus to set sentries around our camp, Jean-Louis and me cleaned our weapons and reloaded them before laying down under a pine tree.

Not the softest bed I'd slept in, but I was tired.

I also realized that my hands were shaking, something that hadn't happened during the fighting. But I reined in the feelings I'd had, the anxiety and the fear, and remembered the hate I'd felt after seeing those poor murdered captives.

The image of that little boy was stuck in my mind and wouldn't go away. Somewhere in Texas, there was a father that felt about that boy the way I felt about Little Ed.

Tomorrow.

I would be ready when we caught up with his murderers.

***

Yesterday's fight had been a confused running gunfight, but General Huston had a different plan in mind.

"We are about 400 all told," he said, "and my spies tell me there are a thousand or more of the enemy, but Gentlemen, they won't stand before our rifles.

"I propose to ride until my spies make contact with their pickets, then dismount and fight as infantry. Pick good men to be your horse-holders, because when we break their line I'll want you to remount and pursue. Captain Hays, I shall depend upon your Rangers to stop them if they try to surround us. Are they up to the task, Sir?"

Jack assured him that they were, and after the general finished talking we headed back for our men.

Mine were camped next to Ed's, seeing as how we'd ridden together the day before. He stopped me as we got closer and said, "I'll want your men with mine today if you don't mind, Jake"

I nodded. General Huston, who'd been army commander at one point and might still be for all I knowed, was an unknown, but I could count on Ed Burleson.

***

Our joint companies ended up behind some others.

I didn't see the rangers, but I figured they were either up front or off doing what the general wanted.

The sun was barely above the treetops when the fight started, and this time it was Texian rifles mixed in with the screeching and whooping of the Comanches.

The crackle started somewhere ahead of us and spread to both sides, what the army calls flanks. After a bit, I noticed that some of the shooting was coming from revolvers so either the Indians had started to surround us or the rangers had got impatient.

I didn't figure it mattered.

I was in the middle of our line of riflemen, with Jean-Louis off to the left flank and Gus over on the right, when I saw my first Comanche of the day. Proud he was, all painted up, and with a headdress that sported horns and a long tail. He was waving a lance and hollering something, maybe challenging somebody to fight, when I shot him.

That .54 caliber bullet flipped him backwards off his horse and his proud bonnet went off in a different direction. I knowed right away that he wouldn't need it, but there was a small grove of trees nearby and the way we were going put me off to his left.

I had thought to scalp the ones I killed, but I could see that there would be no time for this one.

But somebody would, unless they came up and hauled him away first.

I reloaded and kept moving, firing when I saw a target, and now and then looking at my company spread out on either side. I saw Jean-Louis just as he shot an Indian, so I knowed he was unwounded. Gus was somewhere on the other side of the trees, but I heard rifles crack from over there so I figured he was doing what he ought to.

And that was the way it went.

Now and again, when we crossed a creek, I stopped to drink, dunk my head and wipe off my face, and swab out my rifle barrel. And after every stop, I went right back to advancing.

The general was right, in that we broke their line, but I reckon he didn't know Comanches. They just vanished.

One minute they were there shooting arrows at us, the next they were gone, with only the sound of fading hoofbeats to tell us what had happened.

And just like the day before, as soon as the fighting slowed down, men started searching the bodies. Others collected abandoned loot, and some began rounding up horses.

I was with Jean-Louis and Gus, looking for the herd we'd lost when they raided Linnville, when we spotted them.

Not loose now; they were being herded south, back in the direction we'd come from, and a big man with a thick red beard seemed to be in charge. We rode over to thank them for rounding them up for us, but that ruffian had other ideas.

"We lost everything in the raids, just like you," he said. "You lost these when the Injuns stole 'em, if they were ever yours in the first place, and now we've stole 'em back. I reckon they're ours now."

I managed to grab Jean-Louis before he could pull his pistol, but for a minute I was worried. He didn't want to stop, but half a dozen others had come up to Redbeard by then and their rifles were pointed kind of loosely in our direction.

"Nothing we can do here, Jean-Louis. Maybe the general can help." Meantime, Gus looked at that man with the beard. "Don't I know you?" he asked.

"Nope. And if you think you do, why, you just need to think again. We fought the Indians and now that we've rounded up these horses, we mean to have them. You boys can always round up more, unless you decide to make a bad mistake. Being as there was a fight and nobody knows who kilt who, I reckon you'd best go about your business and leave us to ours."

***

We found General Huston, but he brushed us off. Seemed like writing his report of how he'd won the fight all by his lonesome was more important.

We ran into Ed Burleson right after that and told him what had happened.

"Boys, I wish there was something we could do. But the general intends to go after them again tomorrow, and he's smart enough to know that letting a fight break out among his men is about the worst thing that could happen."

"He'll do it without me, then, Ed, and that bunch of thieves won't be there either!"

"I know how you feel, Jean-Louis. Jake, what about you?"

"We're partners, Ed. We might be able to catch the thieves if we start now. Last time they surprised us, but that won't happen again.

"I never did get a Comanche scalp, so I'm right sorry to leave, but we've got families to think of. We worked for those horses and I don't feel right about that bunch of thieves just walking off with our property!"

"I wouldn't worry about that Comanche scalp, Jake," Ed said. "This isn't the end of it. They won't stop as long as there's a single one of them still alive."

We never caught up with the thieves. There were just too many tracks, all mixed in together, and the ones we followed turned out to belong to somebody else, but I did find my two apprentices.

We rejoined our families and headed for home.

Funny thing, though. I finally found out the name of the man who'd stolen our horses. We were busy at the time, Jean-Louis and me, so we couldn't just go off after him, and by the time we caught up he was already dead. Somebody had snuck in during the night and cut his throat from ear to ear.

I knowed I hadn't done it, and since Jean-Louis was with me, he hadn't either. But I had my suspicions.

A month later, I finished the rifle I'd started making right after I heard about what had happened to that man. I decorated it special, using Mexican silver whenever possible instead of brass.

And when I went down to hand it to him in person, Gus was right happy to see it.

The End

Made in the USA
San Bernardino, CA
06 June 2020